mine

mine

a novel by Katie Crawford

Deeds Publishing | Atlanta

Published by Deeds Publishing in Athens, GA
www.deedspublishing.com

Printed in The United States of America

Library of Congress Cataloging-in-Publications Data is available upon request.

ISBN 978-1-944193-22-5

Books are available in quantity for promotional or premium use. For information, email info@deedspublishing.com.

Cover and book design by Mark Babcock

First Edition, 2016

10 9 8 7 6 5 4 3 2 1

Dedicated to my wonderful parents, Martin and Bonnie Lentz.
Thank you for always telling me stories.

mine

adjective \'mīn\

1. that which belongs to me
2. to search for something valuable
3. a subterranean passage under enemy territory

1

They had been relegated to the front stoop, told in no uncertain terms that they were to stay out, Maggie, eight, Janie, six and a half. The cloudless fall day was cool, a reminder of the brittle Pennsylvania mountain cold soon to come. Their mama had been shrieking in the back room all morning.

"Don't worry," said their Daddy softly. "All that yelling is just Mama bringing you a new baby brother or sister."

"Does it hurt her, Daddy?" asked Janie.

Daddy blushed. Maggie could still see traces of coal dust trapped in the creases of his freshly shaven face, flecks of blue black that had permanently adhered to his skin. He looked away, speaking to the closed door to Mama's room, "Go play outside, girls. Go on now."

"Can I hold the baby?" Janie called back to him.

Maggie pulled her out the door, whispering, "You're still too little."

It was Sunday, church day, so Daddy was home, smiling and handsome and still smelling like the beer he'd had the night before. The coal mine was still on Sundays, the men home, sitting on porches, gathering in the narrow streets, faces turned towards the sunlight after their week in the dark. That morning, Maggie heard Mama yelling from the porch, "Teresa, come on up, I think it's time!"

Teresa was Mrs. Murphy and she smelled like old cabbage. Mama had delivered both Maggie and Janie at home, Mrs. Murphy by her side. She was the baby lady, the one they called on in the Patch, having nine children herself, all still alive. Some of them were even already grown up. Two of her older boys worked with Daddy in the mine. Her laundry line wrapped around the tiny yard twice, a constant stream of children spilling out of her front door. Mr. Murphy, her husband, was a miner, too. Maggie didn't think she had ever heard him say more than two words.

Maggie didn't like that Mrs. Murphy was going to be the first to hold her beautiful new baby sister. Maggie knew it was going to be a girl. She had drawn pictures of the baby in her notebook at school. Her teacher, Mrs. Jones, had yelled at her for not paying attention, her voice spilling across and spoiling her baby drawing like grape juice on Sunday clothes. Maggie had wanted to tell her about the baby that was coming and about how she and Janie were going to be her second mamas, but she felt her throat get thick and so she put the drawing away. She never even got to finish drawing the eyelashes. She couldn't wait to run her fingers across those little lashes and watch her baby sister laugh, and laugh, and laugh.

Maggie carried in her face a combination of the unique traits of prior generations. From the time she was a baby, people would stop and stare at her, men, women, young, and old. Her hair, like her Mama's, was deep black, thick, heavy on her shoulders and around her wide face. Her dark eyes matched her Daddy's. She was taller than most girls her age, angular and strong, unlike her sister Janie, who was shorter, softer. She was darker too, her skin always a rich honey color made all the more striking by her constant proximity to Janie who was pale like her Mama, like most of the boys and girls they knew. Maggie and Janie got used to the stares. Maggie would stare right back until the other person was forced to look away.

"That girl is going to be trouble," they used to whistle to her Daddy from the time she was small.

Janie's face was more familiar, common. Her skin was fair, scattered with freckles, her hair not quite red enough to draw attention. Janie knew her sister Maggie was beautiful. She knew it was the kind of beauty that people couldn't help but stare at, wonder where it came from, the kind of beauty that made people whisper, made people wait and watch.

Maggie could never remember when she first realized Mama wasn't shrieking anymore. All she could remember was Janie's tiny hand going all sweaty when Mrs. Murphy yelled for Daddy to come into the room. Maggie expected to see Daddy and her new baby all dressed up in pink, but somehow Janie knew better.

When Daddy did come out he was ashen, his handsome boasting face transformed. He told them all to sit at the table and bow their heads.

"The good Lord took her. She is in heaven now, with the other angels."

"Mama?" Maggie whimpered.

"No, not Mama...the baby girl. You can come and say goodbye."

"It's a baby girl?" Maggie asked.

Daddy could only shake his head yes.

When Daddy took them in to see her, Mama was in bed, perfectly still in her grief, withered, holding a pile of white in her lap. Mrs. Murphy was in the corner taking care of the mess. Mama stared, not uttering a word or even trying to hold onto their baby. Maggie huddled in the corner, afraid of seeing their baby sister, but even more terrified by the blank look in her Mama's eyes. Mama did not call her daughters forward. But Janie walked right over to their baby sister, kissed her, ran her fingers over her lifeless face and hushed her softly as though she were still a writhing newborn. She put one of her tiny hands gently on the baby's cheek and the other on top of Mama's, patting her softly. Daddy finally had to carry her away.

He sent them outside. They sat on the porch side by side, strangely still, Janie's warm hand now finding Maggie's. Bit by bit, word spread around the Patch that Mama's baby was born dead and neighbors started showing up with food and beer and kisses.

Someone went to get the priest. Janie and Maggie were sent to their room upstairs. They huddled under their quilt playing with their own baby dolls.

When the priest arrived at the house, he was with Mr. McNichols, the undertaker. A hush came over the throng of neighbors who had gathered on the porch. Maggie pressed her face against the glass of the tiny window in their room. The priest went inside and came out quickly with Mrs. Murphy. She was holding the bundle of white that was their baby. They piled quickly into the car and left, the crowd still hushed.

Only then did Mama start to grieve. It was a sound like no other Maggie had ever heard. Janie covered her ears and crawled under the quilt, but Maggie felt compelled to listen, letting her mother's wail penetrate her completely, as though her veins would now permanently carry the color of her mother's suffering.

2

Their Mama never was herself again. That's what everyone who knew her said. She went quiet, mumbling her own secret language of despair. They waited for her to emerge, thinking that one day she would come back to them, but she never did. She sat in a chair by the window, eyes vacant, open, and yet blind to those around her—the neighborhood women who quietly arrived each morning to help get her dressed, their Daddy, who forced himself to take her hands each night, to lift her from her chair to walk her to their bedroom to sleep. Her once beautiful eyes stayed blind to her babies too, to Maggie and Janie. After a while no one expected anything more. Sometimes at night Maggie would dream that her Mama was singing over the kitchen sink, her voice clear and pretty.

It was 1947. The war had been over for two years. Truman was president. Somewhere in the world, good had triumphed over evil, but not much had changed in their own coal patch. One hundred and eleven coal miners died that year in a mine explosion in Illinois. That news, even more than the horrors of the Nazis, made their skin tingle. Jackie Robinson, a black man, had signed on with the Brooklyn Dodgers. Boys and girls her age were dreaming about Clarke Gable, Judy Garland, Hollywood, but not Maggie. She was left to only wish for her Mama to sing like she used to instead of making her crazy noises.

Mama was lost, hidden somewhere deep inside her familiar shell of a body. Maggie kept her distance, circling the area where Mama sat, skirting around her presence as though she were entrapped by an electrically charged fence. But Janie was undeterred by this invisible border. Maggie used to catch her sitting at Mama's feet talking to her, saying the words for both of them.

"Mama, I made up a real nice game for my dolls to play and I'm going to teach it to Maggie."

"Sure you will Janie dear, do you want Mama to help you play?"

"No Mama, that's okay I can do it myself. I sure am a big girl aren't I?"

"Sure you are Janie, you're Mama's sweet girl."

Maggie couldn't stand watching this kind of make believe. She wanted to scream at Janie that Mama didn't care about her games or her dolls, that there was no Mama any more. She threw herself into keeping house to make up for her shame at not wanting to even look at her Mama. She learned how to heat the dented tea kettle, how to sweep the dust into the dustpan with one hand, how to cook a can of soup. She recognized the particular, dank smell of dirty children on her own skin and she learned how to keep herself and Janie clean.

At night, Janie would brush her Mama's hair, listening thoughtfully to her rambling, repeating her name.

Daddy left them that year, too. He made sure to show his face at the supper table while one of the neighborhood women took their turn feeding them. The rest of the time he was in the mine or down at the bar. Rumor had it that he even had a girlfriend. One of the boys in the neighborhood told Maggie he saw her once, said he snuck into the back of the bar and watched her Daddy sing. He said this woman of Daddy's had blond hair. Maggie wished he had never told her that one detail. Her Mama's hair was dark and thick, her only vanity among the ordinary. Maggie couldn't even trick herself into thinking that maybe her Daddy was pretending this other lady was Mama.

At school the teachers were nicer to Maggie for a while after they found out what happened. Once, Mrs. Jones even let her stay after school and organize her desk. She loved putting all the pens in order and dusting off the wooden top. Mrs. Jones gave her a nickel and said she was a great worker. She wanted to cry she felt so happy. But Mrs. Jones never asked her to stay again after that. It was like, "Crazy Mama earns you one afternoon and a nickel." Even though she knew she shouldn't, she used to think about what it would be like if her Daddy died. Crazy Mama and dead Daddy were probably worth a dime at least. After a while though, Mama being crazy didn't warrant any special favors. Maggie and Janie became the girls with the Mama who was "funny".

Two weeks before Maggie's ninth birthday, Mama stopped her rocking and crazy noises and went still and silent. Maggie was sitting at the kitchen table and the shock of the sudden stillness made her look up. Mama's hair lay softly on her shoulders and her face appeared full of thought. That was to be her Mama's parting gift, for Maggie would believe throughout her life that even in death one could still dream.

Janie was sitting beside her Mama when it happened, softly humming, unaware that she was gone. Maggie took her sister by the hand.

"Come on, come next door with me. Daddy wanted me to ask Mrs. Murphy something."

"You go. I'll stay here with Mama."

"Come with me. Daddy said so."

Janie got up reluctantly, Maggie pulling her out the front door before she had a chance to look back at Mama's face.

When they got to Mrs. Murphy's, Janie ran inside first. Maggie stood on the porch and gestured to Mrs. Murphy to come out.

"I think my mother died. Please don't tell my sister. Please keep her here."

Mrs. Murphy put her hand over her mouth. She called for her oldest girl to run to get the doctor. She sent her son down to the mine to get Daddy.

She pulled Maggie into her arms. She smelled like her children, like burnt toast, like bacon fat, white soap. She smelled nothing like Maggie's mama.

When the doctor finally got there he said something about their Mama's heart giving out, which made Maggie want to call him a dope because of course her heart gave out. She didn't need a stethoscope and a fancy black bag to know that. Whose heart wouldn't give out after all her Mama had been through?

Janie sat in a corner of Mrs. Murphy's house sucking her thumb. With the other hand she rubbed the fabric on the hem of her dress between her fingers producing a steady rhythm of soft noise that sounded like *hush*.

Mrs. Murphy kept them inside while they carried her Mama out. Later on, Daddy came to get them.

They walked back to their house and he sat them on the porch. Maggie had a brief moment of hope while her Daddy dug his fingers into his pockets, restlessly tapping his foot on the worn porch steps.

Maybe she didn't die. Maybe she went to sleep and they are going to keep her at the hospital until she wakes up. Maybe, she is just sleeping.

She pictured her Mama waking from a long nap, stretching her arms towards the sunlight, shaking out her dark hair. The words finally left Daddy.

"Your Mama died today. The doctor said her heart stopped beating. She is in heaven now." He wanted to say more, but his voice broke. He crouched down on the porch and put his arms around them, his face still black from the mine. His tears made tiny rivers of silt down his cheeks.

The funeral was on a Monday. Mrs. Murphy came over in the morning to make sure they were dressed neatly, hair combed. Daddy's men carried Mama's coffin into the church. It stayed closed. Janie held tight to Maggie throughout the service.

When they put her Mama in the ground Janie pulled Maggie down so she could whisper in her ear.

"If Mama is going up to heaven, why are they burying her here in the ground, under all that dirt?"

"Her soul—her soul went to heaven. Her body stays here."

"Alone? In the dirt?" Janie whimpered.

"Shhh," Maggie could only answer.

The neighbors used the day as an excuse to get good and drunk and her Daddy never came home that night. Mrs. Murphy fell asleep in Mama's rocker. Janie stayed up waiting for Daddy at the edge of the stairs with her baby dolls helping her to keep vigil. Maggie couldn't stand the sight of her sitting there alone and so finally she said that she could come and sleep with her and that yes she could bring her filthy little dolls, too. The next day their Daddy showed up looking gray and guilty. Janie hugged him, but Maggie eyed him coolly from the stairs. It was to Maggie that he made his excuses.

"I was out walking with the men last night. You know I miss your Mama." Maggie walked away leaving Janie to fill the silence she left behind.

It was two weeks later, on her birthday, that Maggie made her wish. Mrs. Murphy baked her a cake and Daddy was actually home. Daddy gave her a doll wrapped in plastic that had blond hair and eyes that opened and closed. Maggie recognized it right away from the five and dime. The dolls held court at the counter along with the plastic roses filled with perfume. They were apology presents—the kind you buy when you realize you forgot your little girl's birth-day or to make up with your sweetheart because you stayed out all night. Maggie knew at least five other girls in the patch toting around the same pathetic, plastic baby. When she opened it she was so disappointed she almost cried. She had been hoping for a pair of shoes with a heel, like the kind she saw girls in the movies wearing. She knew Daddy didn't know her shoe size, let alone what kind of shoes the girls were wearing those days, but somehow she'd convinced herself that he would figure it out, that he would even know to get the kind with the bow on the tip.

He would leave the bar early one night, passing up offers of another round and announce to the men that he had to go and get his daughter Maggie a new pair of shoes because, after all, nine was special. After Maggie opened the doll she managed a thank you and a kiss, but her Daddy knew. His face darkened and he asked for Mrs. Murphy to bring the cake. They struggled through "Happy Birthday," Maggie's mother's voice achingly absent for the first time. Maggie wanted to put her head down on the table and weep. She wanted Daddy to pick her up like she was still a baby and tell her how sorry he was that her Mama wasn't here anymore. She wanted him to tell her that it was going to be ok. He said nothing. The cake stuck in Maggie's throat. She shoveled it in anyway to stop her tears.

Later on that night Janie gave her a package wrapped in colored paper. There was a card too that said, "Dear Maggie, I love you, you are the best sister." Inside was a book Janie had made herself.

"It's a diary," Janie said, "You can write down anything you want in it and no one is allowed to read it."

Maggie hugged Janie and told her she loved it. She told Janie she was going to write about her boyfriends in it, which made Janie laugh. But even at nine, she knew she would leave those pages blank, void of any history or reflection. Maggie didn't plan on looking back, didn't plan on ever needing to look back. Janie alone would be her oracle of this place, this past. Maggie didn't count on losing her or on having to remember—a word she would come to utter almost like a prayer.

3

Theirs was a coal patch. A collection of houses in the shadow of the breaker, meant to hold men, workers, mostly Irish but some Poles and Italians too. Everything about these shacks' construction spoke of temporary conditions; even the porches weren't built wide enough to truly sit on, like the background set of a stage play. But somewhere along the line the men's families came, too. The women managed to stitch together a daily existence despite incessant pregnancy and the thin film of black coal dust that blanketed everything: the clothes, the babies, the small gardens they planted to help make ends meet. Though nothing could compare to the blackness of the men, their hands, their faces, their clothes, the black bile they inevitably coughed up from their lungs.

This was where Maggie and Janie grew up. "Poor souls," people would nod as they walked by their house. Despite Maggie's efforts, she and Janie wore the mark of motherless children. Their only comfort was that theirs was a town of poor souls: one legged miners crippled on the job, returning to the hole since there was nothing else for them to do, daddies coughing up so much black that they could barely stand, young mamas with so many needy babies and more that kept coming. All this mandated by the Lord. The parish priests blessed each one in baptism, praised hard work (the coal company owners kept their coffers full), decried their drunken fathers, and told them all to look to the Lord. But oh where to look? They say that coal dust gets in your blood, that it binds you to the anthracite rich earth at your feet. That's why people never leave. That's why those temporary coal towns held fast to generations. But not to Maggie. Every day she would envision as a hazy memory. This would be her past.

Perhaps it was numbers, simply numbers that first took Maggie out and away from her Janie. Maggie endlessly copied the multiplication tables, delighting in their continuous patterns. She loved the balance of making change. But for Janie, the times tables left her little hands covered in black pencil dust, a paper full of eraser marks dotted with her silent tears, testimony to her effort and failure.

Words eluded her, too. She would find them jumbled across the pages of her favorite stories, stories her mother and later Maggie read to her. She would run her fingers over their scattered forms, desperately trying to make sense of their order. When the teacher called on her she would pray for an answer to appear.

Maggie decided her skill with numbers was a gift from her mother. By the time she was eleven, she'd realized that left to his own devices, Daddy would drink away his paycheck by sunup on Saturday, leaving nothing for food. Maggie took to meeting him at the mine gates on payday, shaming him into handing over his check in front of the other men. She would give him his drinking money and even walked into the bar once to tell Davey the bartender that he was to extend her father no credit.

Daddy still managed to get drunk. The men loved her Daddy. The booze would make him smile and sing out loud. He knew the words to all their favorite songs and no matter how drunk he got, his voice stayed clear and soulful. When he came staggering home at night, he would wake them to tell them how much he loved them, how they were a gift from the angels. Later there would be the vomit, the soiled clothes, and the shame. Maggie would scrub the sink and soak the clothes, but she would not look Daddy in the eye.

There were always tears the day after a night of hard drinking and promises, heartfelt promises that they all knew Daddy could never keep. Still, Janie would hold his hand and listen, forever willing to restore her faith.

Maggie was sixteen when she got her own job working the cash register at the bakery in town. She never made a mistake, challenging herself to add up the figures in her head as fast as the order came in. She squeezed in a few hours before and after school, spending her days smelling like a sticky bun. She loved the work, counting out the change into people's hands, placing the sweets gently onto the waxed tissue paper, securely tying the white cardboard box with string. She even loved washing down the stacks of trays at the end of the day, loved that every item in the bakery had a designated purpose and space, loved the order and predictability so absent from her own home. She washed her apron every night in the sink at their house, laying it flat on the kitchen table to dry overnight without wrinkles.

Maggie half-heartedly tried to get Janie to apply for a job there too, but she knew Janie didn't want to be anywhere near a cash register. Maggie imagined having to cover for her, to hide her sister's mistakes. Janie didn't like being at home alone after school without Maggie and so when a neighbor woman told them they were looking for a cleaning lady down at the priests' home, Maggie encouraged Janie to go apply. She thought, at the very least, her sister would be safe there, protected from scorn.

It was in the morning while working at the bakery that Maggie met Joseph. He was seventeen, one year older than Maggie, but had left school at fourteen to go work in the mine. They had both grown up in the Patch and they were later to recall the multitude of small exchanges they had shared over time. Joseph remembered the day her baby sister died. He'd helped the men carry her Daddy to their front porch countless times from the bar. He'd been witness to much of her history and yet puberty makes strangers out of everyone.

He came in and ordered a box of sticky buns, surrounded by his friends, young boys who left school to work in the mines too, filled with youthful swagger. Joseph was clearly their leader. As she handed him the package he continued to look at her, his face painfully handsome. Maggie averted her eyes, tried to ignore the rush of warmth in the pit of her stomach.

"I know you. You're Maggie Coyle."

"I am. Can I help you with something else?" she asked coldly.

"No. I'm Joseph. I know you—your Daddy, too. And your sister, Janie."

Maggie said nothing.

"Thank you," he smiled and left.

Joseph was there every morning from that day on. He was there to meet her when her shift ended. He was in church, finding a seat in the pew behind her. He was walking up the road with Janie on her way home from the priests' home, making her little sister laugh and smile in a way that no one else could. He was on the front porch the nights he knew that her Daddy wasn't coming home at all—Daddy had indeed found a lady friend in town. And soon, without ceremony, he was upstairs in bed with Maggie, the bed she had always shared with Janie. Janie quietly left to sleep downstairs.

For Maggie yes, there was desire; the cotton shirt washed countless times by Joseph's mother infused with his own strong scent, his mouth eager, smelling pleasantly of cigarettes and beer, his hands tracing her skin. There was desire, but then afterwards there was always contempt, contempt and fear. Fear that she was pregnant despite the precautions that Joseph swore to take. Maggie would cover herself quickly with the tossed sheets and ask him to leave, a sign Joseph took as modesty and fear of getting caught, but truly Maggie wanted him out.

She would spend the night awake, promising that if she got her period this month it would be the last time she ever let him back into her bed. She would marvel at how quickly desire could turn to hate and then back again as she inevitably found herself leading him back upstairs another night. What scared her most is that no one objected, not Janie, not the neighbors, women who had known her Mama, who had seen Joseph leave at dawn on countless mornings— not even her Daddy, who in time surely came to understand what was happening. Maggie Coyle sleeping with a seventeen-year-old miner, risking pregnancy every month was to be expected. That is what left her afraid.

Janie walked to the priests' house directly after school every day. She had her own routine. She was a hard worker. The bathrooms gleamed, the sheets were ironed, the furniture polished, free of any trace of dust. Father James said little to her, but took note that nothing was stolen.

Janie loved being able to complete a job so thoroughly and well, especially after a day at school where everything was a struggle and she couldn't explain why. At first, it was only Father James, already deep into his eighties, sleeping away most of the day. Janie snuck in when she could to change his sheets and gather his laundry.

Once she started working, she realized how little time she had ever spent away from Maggie. To be alone with her own thoughts for a few hours was a novelty. Sometimes her daydreams were so vivid that when she came home at night she felt like she was bursting with news for Maggie. She would quickly realize she had nothing to tell, nothing at all.

Janie prayed often and everywhere. She prayed to her Mama and her Mama's baby. She prayed to the saints and memorized their stories. She prayed to Jesus and felt that she knew him well. When she looked into his eyes in the paintings in the priests' home and at church, she saw a man trying to do right in a world of suffering. She believed she and Jesus would get along just fine.

Janie's faith was her own and while she went to church on Sundays she didn't feel like she needed Father James' guidance to find her path to the Lord. She felt Jesus walking with her every step of the way. While she never prayed for his intervention, she was forever mindful that he was indeed by her side, witness to her world.

Father Timothy arrived in the spring, the same day that Janie turned fifteen. Janie was startled to see someone sitting by the window in the vacant room down the hall from Father James' room. Father Timothy looked up as she entered the room, equally surprised. He was a young man whose hair had gone thin early. He somehow managed to carry the face of a boy in a body that looked deep into middle age. His voice was soft and low when he stood to introduce himself and Janie thought at once how it would never carry to the back of the church on Sundays.

"I'm so sorry—I didn't know anyone was in here," Janie sputtered.

"I'm sorry, too," Father Timothy said, moving away from the unmade bed. "I just got here this morning. I'm Father Timothy. I was sent to help out Father James. I'm the new priest here. Father James said this would be my room."

"I didn't know—I'm sorry. I'll get it ready right away."

"Thank you. What's your name?"

"Janie Coyle."

"Nice to meet you, Janie."

"Nice to meet you too, Father."

"How old are you? I mean—did you come here from school?" he asked quietly.

"I'm fourteen- fifteen. I turned fifteen today," Janie blushed, embarrassed to have shared this.

"Happy birthday."

"Thank you," Janie answered. An awkward silence followed.

Father Timothy spoke first, "Well, I'm happy to have met you on your birthday."

"Thank you, Father. I'll get your room ready."

"Thank you Janie," he answered quietly, each word measured precisely, lacking even the hint of inflection, emotion.

She hurried out of his room to go and gather fresh bedding. While Father Timothy had spoken to her, Janie had wondered what it was that seemed to be suffocating him so completely. It wasn't piety, or fear, or even nervousness. As she pulled the sheets tight across his single bed, she realized she recognized his particular burden well, had seen it many times before. She knew before the gossip even reached her that Father Timothy was a shamed man.

There was lots of talk as to why Father Timothy had found his way to their church, all of it whispered and none of it good. Some said that he came from a church in California and that he'd slept with a married woman there, that as punishment he'd been sent to the most godforsaken place on Earth, their coal patch. Some said it was boys that he liked. Some said he'd had a baby with a sister and that they had sent their love child off with missionaries to Africa. Come Sunday no one had a word to say. They would cross themselves and greet Father Timothy as if he was the Pope himself. Janie felt herself rooting for him silently from the pew. His voice never rose above a mumble, and small beads of sweat would gather slowly across his brow as the service went on, his eyes finding only the ceiling.

On Monday, when she would come to clean she would always find him sitting by the window in the front hall. He would stand to greet her, and she would marvel at how his face could be so transformed once he was away from the pulpit, again like a young man.

One afternoon, Father Timothy approached her as she was on her way upstairs to clean the bedrooms.

"Do you like coffee? I am about to make myself some," his voice startled her.

"Yes," she found herself saying even though she had never tried coffee in her life.

"I'll make you a cup then," he answered.

"No, don't go to the trouble, it's ok—I'm fine," Janie answered quickly, awkwardly.

"I'd like to make you some coffee. It's really no trouble," he answered quietly.

"Ok then, thank you," Janie mumbled and then hurried upstairs. She could hear him downstairs in the kitchen, running the water, turning on the stove.

She came downstairs after cleaning the bedrooms and found the cup waiting for her in the kitchen, a saucer on top to keep it hot, complete with a container of cream and sugar. Father Timothy had even left a molasses cookie baked by the nuns on the side. The sight of the white china cup, prepared for her, made her chest ache with an unexpected sadness. Not since her Mama had made her tea as a little girl had anyone prepared something for her, a warm drink solely to enjoy. So much of the food she had been served over the years had been by women who were doing their Christian duty and no matter how well intentioned, the food they offered was always taken from their own families, cooked out of righteous obligation.

Janie often made her Daddy tea, but it was a drink of necessity, a drink to sober up, a drink to help the nausea, a drink to put something in his stomach. But this single cup for her was something new. She added the cream and sugar sparingly and took a sip while still standing. It was awful. She forced herself to drink it down and took it into the kitchen and washed the cup and put it away. Before she left, she found Father Timothy still by the window.

"Thank you," Janie shyly pushed the words from her lips.

Father Timothy looked up, startled from his reverie.

"For the coffee. Thank you," she repeated.

"Yes. I'll see you tomorrow."

He watched her walk away. From that day on, there was always coffee. It would be waiting for her when she arrived. In time, she came to like its bitter taste, looked forward to it on her way to work. She still drank it while standing in the kitchen, savoring the last crumbs of the cookie, grateful for this small act of unsolicited kindness. Every day she would thank Father Timothy who would nod and smile and return his gaze to the window.

4

Graduation in the Patch was a cruel joke. The girls would dress up in white dresses and the boys in coats and ties and there would be long speeches by teachers and the principal about how this year's graduating class was the class of the future and how the opportunities for their success were endless. On that day Maggie thought the senior girls beautiful and the boys brilliant, lucky enough to have made it to graduation day without dropping out to make money at the mines or because they got a girl into "trouble". There was either going to be a wedding—short and sad in the side chapel with no white dress or cake or flowers, or even worse some poor girl was going to take a vacation with the sisters for a little while. These girls always came back looking pale and puffy and oh so sad at having lost their baby, and their lover, and their chance at wearing a white dress and being part of the class of the future, even for one day.

After graduation, those same beautiful girls in white dresses seemed again ordinary, hanging around the Patch waiting for someone to ask them to marry them or working at the drugstore or the movie house. Every once in a while some girl would get a job as a secretary or a bank teller down in Ashland and the whole Patch would have to hear for weeks from their mothers about how much money they were making and their grand plans for the future. But when you came right down to it, Ashland was really just another small town down the road.

In spring of her senior year, Maggie's teacher announced that they were having a special visitor from Philadelphia join them that day. At 10:30 the classroom door opened and in walked a woman, dressed in a spotless white nurse's uniform. Her name was Miss Brooks and she was a nurse in Philadelphia at Pennsylvania Hospital. She was there to announce an entrance examination for potential nursing students to be given in Harrisburg. The top five students in the state of Pennsylvania would receive full scholarships to attend Pennsylvania Nursing school. She stood at the front of the room and looked calmly out over the sea of faces, confident, detached. She was merely passing through their small town on her way to many more, showing them one possible road out. She seemed to neither hope nor care if any of them followed. Maggie felt her whole body tense up, felt an unexpected rush of warmth to her cheeks, her palms go moist, as if the woman were speaking directly to her. Maggie knew without reason that she would be one of the students chosen. This is how she would get out.

She waited to tell Daddy until he was hungover, the only time he was reliably sober.

"I'm going to take a test in Harrisburg next week. A test to become a nurse, go to nursing school. A lady came to school to tell us about it last week."

Daddy said nothing.

"My teachers all think I should take it—that I have a good chance. There's a scholarship for the girls who score the highest. You wouldn't have to pay for anything. Not even books."

"Where's the school?" Janie asked quietly.

"Philadelphia. Pennsylvania Hospital's nursing school."

"You mean you would go live there?" Janie asked.

"For a while."

"You want to be a nurse?" Daddy finally spoke.

"Yes."

"How you gonna get to Harrisburg?"

"I'm gonna take the bus."

"And if you get in where you gonna live in Philadelphia?"

"They have dorms, rooms for the students. It's part of the scholarship. Like I said you wouldn't have to pay for anything, Daddy."

"That is an evil city."

"I'm taking the exam on Saturday."

"Good luck then." Daddy said nothing more and left the room.

"I hope you get it," Janie could only bring herself to whisper.

Janie walked Maggie to the station the morning of the exam, offering words of encouragement, a thermos of tea, and a well worn, plastic covered prayer card of St. Jude, patron saint of lost causes.

Sudden, unexpected, rare tears, began to run down Maggie's cheeks as the bus approached. Janie looked at her, stunned.

"Are you crying? Are you nervous? Don't be—you are going to do great! It'll be ok," Janie wrapped her arm around her sister.

"Silly. I'm fine," Maggie wiped her eyes and brushed her sister off.

But she cried because she knew this simple act was the first step of betrayal, of leaving. Disemboweled, a word she had come across while studying an old medical book on treating war casualties in the field kept repeating itself in her mind. Their mother's death was like a rebirth for the two sisters; they came into a motherless world fused together like Siamese twins by their grief. Separation would be physically traumatic.

The results came four weeks later. Maggie scored number two in the entire state.

5

Father Timothy tries to forget that the girl, Janie, that he watches so closely now walking up the narrow path is the same age that his sister was then. There had only been the two of them in that house, set so far from the road, the two of them and his father, her stepfather, their mother long gone. "Felled by illness," he had once heard someone say which made him think of his mother as a tree, graceful and enormous, in full bloom when she was suddenly hacked to the ground, hacked to death by an unknown disease, pestilence. He does not remember her face. His half sister, sharing only their mother, aptly named Faith, seven years older, is the one who takes care of him, gets him off to school, washes his clothes, takes him down to church on Sunday. She teaches him the rosary, tells him Jesus was a shepherd, that they are eternally part of his flock. She collects pieces of old newspapers put out by the road when she walks him to school. At night she shows him how to cut rows of paper dolls.

"They look like a row of angels," he says.

"Don't they just? Let's name them. This can be the Mama angel."

They would spend hours together passing the paper figures back and forth, the scattered print across their faces becoming recognizable as features, an eye, a mouth, a smile. As darkness came and their daddy threatened to come home Faith would fold the dolls neatly and pretend to put them to bed within the pages of the bible. Once, when he had come home early, he found their paper family spread out across the floor.

He tossed them into the fire.

"You gonna make him a faggot you keep playing girl games with him like this..."

Timothy watched quietly as the flames took hold, his angels' legs and arms curling upwards meeting a line of burning faces.

Faith came to see him in bed that night.

"What's a faggot?" he asked quietly.

"Don't listen to him."

"What is it? What does he think is gonna happen to me?"

"A faggot is a man who loves men."

"I'm not one of them. I don't love any man."

"Shhh.... Come on now. Go to sleep."

On Saturdays, when his father was home, when the hours stretched on dangerously, Faith would send Timothy outside, telling him to go look at the birds out back, to wait until she came to get him, to guard the feeders against the squirrels, to not take his eyes off those feeders, to not turn back towards the house. His daddy would merely scream at him to get the hell out.

He did as he was told, waiting for Faith to come and collect him from his post. He would gather a small pile of rocks beside him, taking aim at the brazen squirrels.

"I want to go in, I'm getting cold," he would whine to her when she finally came out.

Faith would come and sit down, her face oddly blotched, her lips already blue with cold, shivering in whatever cover she had hastily thrown on.

"Just sit with me a minute—I think he's almost asleep. Can you tell me the name of that tiny bird again? The black and white one?"

"That's a chickadee. Oh look, the blue jay came and scared it off. It'll be back though."

The day he saw them he had been out back for what seemed like hours. His hands were cold even though he had sat on them for most of the time. He picked up a rock from his pile, focusing on an especially fat squirrel, making its way up the tree to the suet block. He took aim. When the squirrel dropped he stood up quickly, rushing to find its body at the base of the tree. It was quivering in its final moments of life. He stepped on it to make it still. Picking it up he raced inside to show Faith, for surely this warranted an interruption. Even his Daddy would be amazed.

He would never know why he slowed his pace as he approached the front door, why he turned the lock so quietly, balancing the lifeless body of the squirrel in one hand, already stained with blood and small tufts of grey fur.

It would have been better if her eyes had been closed, but they were open, taking in the cracked ceiling above her while his Daddy's shocking figure of bare flesh crushed her completely. When she saw him, her eyes came alive again in terror. She put a finger to her lips.

When she came for him out back he had already tossed the body of the squirrel deep into the woods, wiped his hands on the thick grass.

"Don't tell anyone. Promise. He'd kill me, he'd kill us both. Maybe not you, you're his flesh and blood, but me for sure," she said flatly.

"I hate him. I hate that man," he answered, voice cracking.

"You can't hate your own Daddy."

6

They never said much to each other, but seeing Father Timothy every day was enough for Janie to start to feel like he was a part of her life, something she looked forward to, a private world. Silence leaves much to the imagination. Sometimes Father Timothy would have his bible open, working on his sermon. Sometimes he would be outside, filling the bird feeders for the birds he so loved to watch. Together they shared this quiet, orderly existence.

"Good morning, Janie."

"Good morning, Father."

"How's your family?"

"They're good. Thank you."

"It's just your sister and your father at your house?"

"Yes, Father. My mother died some years back."

"I'm so sorry... My mother died when I was young, too."

Janie looked up startled at this admission, "I'm sorry, Father." He had already looked away, turned his eyes to the window, as though watching some memory revealed in its glass.

"It's hard—not having a mother when you're young. I had a sister though, like you do." Father Timothy resisted the urge to say his sister's name.

Janie stood quietly waiting.

He finally spoke again, "What was your mother's name?"

"Her name was Veronica... but everybody called her Bonnie."

"Veronica—for St. Veronica?" he asked softly, hopefully.

Janie shook her head yes.

Father Timothy continued, "I have always loved that story. A man condemned to die, carrying a heavy cross on the way to his own crucifixion. Jesus. And Veronica, this ordinary woman, out of kindness, kindness for a condemned man, wipes his face. Such a simple act, but so brave. Jesus' face appears on the cloth. It becomes a miracle. A simple kindness becomes a miracle."

Janie was transfixed.

"I will pray for her," he said softly and returned to his book. *Faith would have done the same,* he thought. *My sister would have stopped to help a man condemned.*

"Thank you. Thank you, Father," Janie said and left the room.

She went upstairs to clean. She wished she could have asked him his own mother's name, wished she could have kept him talking, but she had felt the hot tears begin to form as soon as her mother's name left her lips. Veronica—like the saint. She wanted to hear him say her mother's name again.

The day it first happened the coffee was there waiting, but Father Timothy was not in his usual spot by the window. Janie went about her tasks, eagerly listening for his footsteps, but there was silence. After she finished her coffee, she made her way upstairs to the bedrooms. Father Timothy sat on the edge of the unmade bed weeping silently.

Janie froze in the doorframe.

"Father Timothy?"

When he looked up and saw her he locked his hands together in his lap, as if in prayer.

"Can I get you something?"

He let his eyes fully rest on the girl before him now. One could still see behind the small rise of her breast, the remnants of childhood.

26

"Father Timothy?" she repeated slowly.

He heard in her voice what he thought was permission. He had done nothing wrong.

"Come in. Come and sit with me a minute," he answered.

Janie would always remind herself that she could have walked away. She could have ignored him—she could have simply gone on back downstairs and started scrubbing the kitchen floor. Maggie would have left. Maggie would have looked the other way. Maggie would not have let some man's trouble bring her down. But Janie did what she had always done, what came naturally, what she did best. She went and sat by his side. He unclenched his fingers and cautiously took her hand.

That was how it began. He waited there each day now. There would be coffee and the empty chair and she would know he was upstairs. At first he only took her hand, but then there was more. Maggie had told her what it was like with Joseph, how he had done everything, how she had said no at first, how it had hurt so badly. She had told Janie how even though she liked it sometimes, she always felt bad afterwards, guilty and sad like she wanted to cry, but for some reason she would let it happen again, even wanted it to happen again even if only for a brief moment. When it hurt, Janie reminded herself that it had hurt for Maggie. When she would feel like crying when it was over, she would remember that Maggie always felt like crying, too. When she would promise herself that it would never happen again and then would find herself climbing back up the stairs, she would understand what it was like for Maggie, too.

Janie would come to wonder why she never spoke up, never told another soul, not even her Maggie. She could have screamed. Though mostly deaf, Father James slept down the hallway. She could have quit. But she didn't. It was hard for her to feel wronged when what was happening was something she ached for so badly, when mere proximity was what she craved night and day. How could she be the victim when the look of remorse, of grief, was always deeper in his eyes? It was his tossed clothes that looked like innocence, shockingly spilled across the floor, not hers. Afterwards he would stand and dress, not looking at her again. She would gather herself and strip the bed to wash the sheets.

She never found out why he was weeping on that first day, the first time he touched her. Once his tears had called her in, they suddenly ran dry.

7

J oseph quietly listened when Maggie told him the news.

"Remember I went and took that test? In Harrisburg?"

"Yeah. I remember," Joseph tensed immediately.

"Well I got it. I got the scholarship. I start in September."

"You mean you're going? You're gonna go?" Joseph could feel his heart begin to race, the same way it did every time he entered the mine. It was Maggie's face that he remembered on the way down every morning, in exact detail, her dark eyes, full, set mouth, the color of her hair against her bare shoulder, the tiny mole at the base of her throat. This ritual cleared his head of fear, calmed his heart, gave him faith that he would emerge safely from underground again.

"Yeah. I'm going. They pay for everything. Isn't that great?"

"How long is it?" he asked steadily, controlling the tremor in his voice.

"Two years." Maggie could see Joseph's face fall. She weakened. She had told herself she would end it now, end it before she went away, tell him not to wait, tell him she would never be back. "It's only two hours away. A bus trip really. I get vacation and weekends. I'll be home a lot."

"What did your Daddy say?"

"Nothing except Philadelphia is an evil city. Can't imagine how it could be more evil than here," she forced a laugh.

"He's right. What did Janie say?"

"Janie's happy for me. She wants me to go...I guess she's the only one who is happy for me."

"That's a lie and you know it—she doesn't want you to go. That girl will be lost here without you."

"Don't say that. Please. She'll be fine. She'll figure it out. I'm going. I want to go."

Joseph said nothing for a minute. He knew he had no choice. He reached out to touch her cheek. "That's great Maggie. I'm real happy for you, too," he smiled.

"I'll be back—a lot."

"I know. I know you will."

The heat that summer was insufferable. Maggie spent more and more time at work and studying at the town library. She carried the heavy stacks of medical books into a corner, poring over their pages, the photographs of disease, of exceptional deformity, ravaged humanity. The eyes in the photographs were blank, listless, beyond shame. She was reminded of when her Daddy took her and Janie to the tiny circus that came to town. Beyond the big tent with the animal acts, there was a smaller enclosed one, a long line leading into its curtained doors—the freak show.

The sisters had held hands as they walked inside. Maggie tasted terror in her mouth. There was the bearded woman, the alligator man whose flesh was raw with disease, the dwarf dressed in doll clothes, face thick with makeup, standing on top of a table so that ticket holders could get a better look. Maggie had pulled Janie through, desperate to escape. That night she had dreamt of witches, black and ghostlike, flying over her roof, their spells evoking horrific transformations. When she awoke in the dark she ran her fingers over her face, her body, reassuring herself that she was unchanged, snuggling close to her sister.

Janie went quiet that summer before Maggie left. She would

come from cleaning the priest's home and go straight to bed, turning the pages of the well worn bible her Mama had left behind. Maggie would listen alone in her room as her sister's voice floated up through the floorboards, like a familiar ghost.

Though I walk in the midst of trouble; yet thou refresh me.

Maggie refused to feel guilty. She would lie restless in bed listening to the recited prayers of the solemn, joyless girl her sister had suddenly become. She would press against the tender spot in her right wrist remembering what it used to be like.

After Maggie's Mama died, when she was about ten and Janie eight, they'd made up a game to pass time one Saturday morning while their daddy slept off another biblical hangover. They would start at the bottom step of their porch and jump out to see how far they would land. Janie always quit by the third step but Maggie was brazen as her Daddy used to say and she would make the final leap from the top step, eliciting shrieks from a terrified Janie. After several flawless leaps, Maggie went to join her sister on the steps.

Her Daddy's angry face appeared at the window and Maggie went to duck but tripped, landing squarely on her right wrist. After hours of leaping fearlessly from the top steps, she'd broken her wrist by tripping on the bottom. She waited two excruciating days before she told her Daddy something was wrong. They put a cast on at the local hospital. When the cast came off, weeks later, her arm looked wizened, like it had been eaten away. Janie could not suppress a gasp of horror. Maggie was terrified despite the doctor's reassurance that it would be ok. He gave her an ointment to apply, which Maggie did religiously.

Her arm quickly returned to looking normal but there always remained a tender spot on her wrist. Whenever she and Janie crossed the street together, Janie would reach for that arm and somehow find that tender spot, holding fast to her sister as they crossed together. Whenever Maggie was anxious, she found that tender spot too, finding comfort in its familiar ache.

8

The sight of the waiting cup of coffee now turned Janie's stomach. She would dump it down the sink quickly.

Inside me there is a life was the thought that followed Janie everywhere that insufferable summer. The weight of it was there while she scrubbed the floor bleach white. It was there while she arranged Father Timothy's cassock on the ironing board, taking care not to scald the collar. It was there in the morning, repeating itself amid the waves of nausea. She knew. She carried the heaviness of her secret everywhere.

She would not go upstairs until she saw Father Timothy outside, quickly gathering his dirty laundry from his room, hastily changing his sheets, all the while listening for the sound of his footsteps on the stairs. She did not want him to touch her, her and her baby again.

"Janie," he said, quietly surprising her from behind while she stood at the sink in the kitchen, his scent hitting her before his words. The brazenness of his proximity outside of his bedroom and even more than that, the sound of her own name coming from his mouth left her briefly stunned.

"Janie, I want..."

She cut him off. She was to never know what it was he wanted at that moment.

"No more," was all she said, her voice strong and clear, her hands quickly, defensively, obviously finding her stomach. She did not recognize her own voice.

He must have known then, known that once more he had gone too far, once more it was time to move on, to leave another place behind, quickly. She was not the first girl to find him alone, find him wanting.

"Will you..." he began in a darker tone.

"No I won't. I won't tell," Janie stopped him. His intentions were brutally clear to her now, but still he continued.

"The thing is—I don't know if I'm the only one, the only one to blame," he answered steadily.

He knew what to say, the memory of his father's venomous words decades ago more ingrained in his skull than any nightly prayer.

I'm not taking the blame for this goddamn it! I don't know whose baby it is—I know you're a whore, a slut like your mother! Get the hell out of my house. You stay away from him, too—if I hear you were back around here you'll both pay for it.

His half sister Faith had left that night. He never saw her again.

His father never touched him. They existed in that house devoid of women, the memory of his mother and of his Faith poorly boxed up, left to rot. At night in bed, Timothy would take out the last chain of paper dolls she had left behind, hidden safely in the bible. He would run his fingers over their faces, comforted that Faith's hands had once gently held this paper family, believing that they carried a certain kind magic.

The local priest, Father Ryan, came and sought him out, hearing about Faith's shameful departure, pregnant by Lord knows who, shaming the man who had provided for her all of these years even though she was not his flesh and blood.

He encouraged Timothy to come to Sunday school, to come to church to seek comfort.

The Lord is my shepherd. I shall not want.

He became an altar boy, methodical in his learning of each service, reliable and exact. Father Ryan began to ask him to come by and help after school; there were always countless tasks that needed tending to. Father Ryan had a hummingbird feeder which he carefully filled with the exact proportions of sugar and water to draw in the tiny bird, miraculous in its pace and size.

"Stand still by the window and you can watch them come in," Father Ryan had told him.

When Timothy felt Father Ryan's warm breath at the base of his neck, quietly having approached him from behind, he felt, in that infinitesimally small moment before terror set in, before Father Ryan's hands made clear his intentions, he had felt happy, happy and safe. He froze and watched the hummingbird approach, its beating wings matching his heart.

Let's pray together and ask the Lord's forgiveness. We have been tempted by Satan again.

Timothy told no one. The two of them, nine year old Timothy and ageless Father Ryan, asked for forgiveness together, bonded in sin. Timothy was eternally grateful that Father Ryan never told his own father about their misdeeds.

He learned from Father Ryan that there was no act, no matter how evil, that the Lord would not forgive as long as one always strived to walk in His path, to seek His forgiveness. The church provided a perpetual road to grace, no matter how far and how frequently we lost our way.

He would walk home from Father Ryan's trembling, the holy man's heavy scent clinging to hidden parts of his skin. It lingered there, a feral, contagious odor, like sin itself.

Timothy joined the priesthood when he was sixteen. Where else could he ever find a home large enough for his memories, his sins?

The rumors that hit the patch when Father Timothy arrived were partly true. He had moved often during his life as a young priest, prodded more by sin than by faith, more by the need to cover his tracks than the need to offer enlightenment. His circuitous, enormously creviced road to salvation had led him to pause briefly here, with Janie.

9

Maggie left that September. They all walked her down to the bus station, Janie, Joseph, Daddy. Maggie looked at Janie, her face, pale and strangely swollen, like another version of herself, heartbroken. Maggie hugged her goodbye and caught the sob that rose without warning in her throat. She would not cry. Grief had been her lifelong companion; she knew well she had to swallow it quickly.

When the bus pulled up it looked to Janie like a living creature, menacing and unchained. She tried to make out the faces looking out its windows, their expressions flat, unreadable. Maggie turned and gave one more wave goodbye and climbed up the bus steps. She did not take a seat by the window as they had hoped.

They all stood waving foolishly, while the bus disappeared, all except Daddy, who remained motionless, eyes fixed squarely on the heavens.

They stood silently, unified by their shock of her seemingly sudden absence. They would be no more stunned if she had vanished into thin air before their eyes. That bus, those strangers, had taken her away. Maggie had chosen to leave.

Daddy spoke first, "I guess your mother would have been happy to see her do this, happy to see her get an education, become a nurse."

Janie shook her head yes, fighting the tears. She knew her Mama wouldn't be proud of what she had done.

"Do you want to go and get a drink, Joseph? Celebrate your freedom?" Daddy laughed. Joseph winced.

"That's ok, Mr. Coyle. You go on. I'll walk Janie home."

"You sure? The girls are going to be smiling all over the Patch when they hear she's gone."

"I'm going to keep them waiting just a little longer," Joseph said.

"All right then. I'll see you tonight, Janie."

"Ok, Daddy."

Janie and Joseph began to walk.

"You ok, Janie?"

"Yeah. How about you?"

Joseph nodded. They were silent, suddenly awkward with Maggie gone.

"Are you going to go visit her?" Janie asked.

"If she asks me to I will, I guess." They walked on for a while in silence. Joseph finally spoke again, "Listen, Janie, let me know if you ever need anything, okay? Just because Maggie's gone doesn't mean you can't ask. Okay? If you're Daddy gets out of hand—anything. If you ever need some extra money—I'd like to help you if you ever need me."

Janie reflexively put her hand on her stomach, ashamed, as though he knew.

"Thank you. I'll be okay."

They walked on together until Janie's house came into sight. The four porch chairs stood empty across the sagging floor, waiting.

10

It took Janie's round belly bulging from her tiny frame for Father James to finally notice. Daddy, clearly aware of the transformation of his daughter, remained silent. Only then did Father James also take note of how she scurried from the room whenever Father Timothy approached. Janie was unversed in deception. One morning as she arrived for work, Father James stopped her at the front door, leading her to his study. He closed the door behind them and motioned for her to sit down in one of the leather chairs.

She had wiped down these chairs countless times, marveling at the intricacies of their wooden frames, winding her rag to a point to eliminate any trace of dust. She would imagine the man who had carved them, the time it must have taken him to make each chair, every detail serving only to further their beauty. What kind of life would a man like that live?

Father James was silent for a moment, breathing heavily before he began, "Janie, I think, after you finish up today, it's best if you don't come back to work anymore given your—your condition. I think it's time to move on. I've talked to the sisters who run the home for unwed mothers. It's not far from here. I have sent girls before, girls like you. They have a place for you there. I think it will be best for you, for the baby, especially since you have no mother at home. The Catholic church will make sure to find your child a home, a home in a strong Catholic family. I will talk to your family." He paused, "I mean I will talk to your father. What has your father said?"

"He hasn't said anything, Father. We haven't... we haven't talked about anything," Janie answered softly.

"Well—it is difficult for a father, I imagine. I will talk to him."

"Thank you."

"Do you understand me now, Janie? After today you are not to come back here. Ever. Even after your baby is born. You will not come back to this house?" He spoke to her as if she were a small child.

Janie shook her head in silent agreement.

Father James continued, "I will let your father know about the home and I will arrange for your transportation there. You do understand that after you have the baby, it will be adopted by another family. You do understand? You will—give this baby up?"

"Yes, I understand. Thank you, Father James," Janie got up to leave quickly. She went and began her work. She waited until Father James was asleep in his room that afternoon, listening for his deep snores. She knew Father Timothy was at church hearing confession, that he would be gone for hours.

She walked up the stairs one last time to his room.

She had cleaned it that morning, dusted every corner, made up the bed with freshly pressed sheets, wiped down the shelves and furniture. She wanted to leave it well taken care of. Father Timothy's bible sat on his desk. She gently opened its pages. A yellowed newspaper chain of paper dolls fell out, floating lightly to the floor like a feather. Janie picked them up to place them back into the bible, but stopped to take a closer look. The paper reminded her of a fan she once had, a rare gift from her Daddy, delicate and veined. She closed the bible and quickly hid the paper dolls under her shirt, the line of figures spread out across her growing belly. She walked back downstairs and left without looking back once.

Father James called Father Timothy into his study that evening. Father Timothy sat in the same place Janie had earlier that day.

"I've arranged for the girl to not come back—she is going to stay with the sisters until the baby is born," he said flatly.

"I—I didn't," Timothy began to answer. Father James put his hand up.

"I've arranged for your transfer. Not right away—in a few weeks time. It's better this way." Timothy shook his head in agreement, recognition.

The two men were silent together for a moment. Father James spoke again, "I know you are a young man and that there is always temptation. It is our calling to continue to fight that temptation, to repent, to ask for forgiveness."

Weary, he added softly, "And who truly knows if you are the one to blame?"

11

Down from Mahanoy and the first girl she meets when she arrives at the dormitory is Katie O'Neil from Shenandoah, down the road from her own hometown. She was also there on scholarship and had scored number four in the state, leading many to joke that perhaps coal dust wasn't so bad for you after all.

Maggie took quickly to her studies. While the other girls complained about the work, the poor cafeteria food, the cold, stark rooms, Maggie marveled at the luxury of only being responsible for studying. She sent frequent, meaningless notes home, and read the notes from Janie, knowing how much effort each word cost her. Joseph's cards were store bought, ornate and flowery, his name neatly printed beneath the card's own scripted message of love. Maggie tossed the letters into the trash as soon as she read them, as though their presence alone could weaken her, bring them closer.

She studied constantly, making endless lists of facts and vocabulary, huddled under a blanket at her small desk in her room while her roommate slept. Her mind was filled with new information, the beginnings of her understanding of the human body, its strength, what made it fail. She would climb into bed exhausted, grateful to be too tired to dream, to let her mind wander home.

But come October, having been gone for only two short months, right before Maggie's first exams, her Daddy turned up outside her dorm, drunk and already practically weeping with remorse. The sight of him filled her with shame. She managed to get the doorman to agree to take him inside to sober up somewhere, somewhere out of sight from her classmates, her teachers. She hurried off to get a soda and some medicine for the nausea which would surely ensue. She knew her Daddy well as a drunk.

When she returned he was already mournful, as expected, telling Maggie he was sorry, that he didn't know how the drink caught up with him so quickly. She noticed that his eyes were heavier and that the sideburns of his thick, dark hair were now tinged with grey. His anguished expression was all too familiar. Maggie was in no mood to make him feel better. She knew her Daddy's visit had to have a darker side. She took him out the back door of the main lobby, pressing money into the doorman's hands for sparing her such disgrace. She walked with her head down to a coffee shop six blocks from school. Daddy followed a few steps behind, like a reprimanded child. She did not speak again until they were safely seated in a booth in the back.

"So what is it, Daddy? What is it that you needed so badly that you had to come all the way down from upstate to ask me? What is it that you are so nervous to tell me that you had to get good and drunk and weepy before you could get the words out? Do you need money or something?"

Daddy watched the words come out of Maggie's mouth. He said nothing for a while.

"It's Janie," he finally said, almost in a whisper.

His words sliced through her brittleness and left her simply afraid.

"What happened to Janie?"

"I don't know what happened—but it's a woman she needs. There were rumors, talk, and all I know is that Janie wouldn't look me in the eye, wouldn't answer my questions. I didn't know what was happening- it's not a father's place to talk about such things. With your mother gone... I need you to call Janie."

41

"Talk about what? Where is Janie? What happened?" Maggie could feel her skin begin to tremble. Her father could not look at her.

"She is staying with the sisters."

Maggie froze, speechless.

Her Daddy finally looked into her eyes, pleadingly, "Will you call her? I'd like you to call her. Please. I brought you lots of change for the call and here," he handed her an envelope. "Inside is the number of where she's staying. She is not really allowed phone calls but I told them she would want to talk to you and with your mother gone, and you here at school they agreed to just this once. I put a little something for you in the envelope, too. Please call her."

He slid the envelope across the table into Maggie's lifeless hands. Maggie said nothing.

"It's good to see you Maggie. I'm sorry I made such a mess of the visit," he stared at the ground.

"I didn't want it to be like this. I wanted to spend some time with you," he paused to look at his watch, "... and here I've already got to go back. My bus leaves in a half hour. I guess it did take me a while to come find you. It's true what they say about this city being an evil place, a bar on every corner," he forced a sheepish smile. Maggie still had not spoken.

They walked in silence to the bus depot, her Daddy occasionally whistling low to fill the awkward space. He kissed her goodbye and left, hurrying her home, saying he didn't like her out here on the streets at dark. Maggie watched him pass through the station doors. She stood motionless, stunned, the crumpled envelope holding the number for Janie clutched in her hand.

She had heard these stories before, stories about girls she knew, quietly leaving to stay with the sisters. Together she and Janie had watched these young girls go, watched them come back as women, sad and serious, their girlhoods evaporated completely, their lives marked eternally by this single journey, their arms empty. And now they had her Janie. Maggie knew what it meant to stay with the sisters.

12

"How did this happen? Who is the father? Does Joseph know? Who did this to you?" Maggie's words came tumbling out as she choked back tears.

Maggie clutched the pay phone and stared out at the people rushing by on their way home from work. She had walked twenty blocks before she found a phone booth that seemed far enough away to receive such news.

Janie's voice on the telephone was unfamiliar.

"This is my mistake, Maggie. Please stop asking me who did this. Promise me you will stop asking. It doesn't matter anyway. It's my fault. I am giving the baby up. I made a mistake."

"But Janie..."

"Please," said Janie softly.

"I won't ask you again. It's ok. It's nobody's business. I won't ask. What are you going to do?"

"I am going to stay here with the sisters until it's time to have the baby. The church is going to find a good family for her and then after I have her, I'm going to go home again to Daddy."

"You said her. You think it's a girl?" Maggie couldn't stop the silent tears pouring down her face. She could only see Mama's baby girl. She could feel fear rising inside of her, like ice water slowly filling her chest.

"I don't know and it doesn't matter anyway," said Janie, her voice faltering for the first time.

"You never even told me there was anyone you liked Janie—not ever."

"Please Maggie!" her voice growing desperate, "Please do me this one favor—you said you wouldn't ask me again about this baby's father! Please—I'm begging you!"

"Ok, ok. It doesn't matter now. It just matters that you are going to be ok," Maggie said holding back her tears. She forced the words to come out of her mouth, "Do you need me to come home?"

Janie answered quickly, strongly, "No. I don't need you to come home. I don't want you to come home. I can't talk anymore. Take care now. I love you."

Janie hung up.

Maggie whispered *I love you* to the cold end of the dead phone. She leaned her head against the dirty glass of the telephone booth and sobbed. She could picture Janie now, placing the unfamiliar phone gently down on the receiver, chin out, forcing herself to be brave. Maggie could see her struggle. How many times had she seen her Janie forced to be so very brave? Each first day of school, climbing the steps to her new classroom, awaiting the ridicule, *Why Janie Coyle you can barely read!*

Every Mothers' Day the other children lined up in church to take a single pink carnation from a large bucket placed at the foot of the altar. They would walk back to the pews to happily hand this gift to their awaiting mothers. Janie and Maggie, flowerless, would walk to the side aisle and light a candle for their mama. Maggie always kept the tears at bay by remembering that her mother would have preferred a handful of dandelions gone wild. *Could there be a better bouquet on Earth than a thousand wishes?* she would say. Maggie could close her eyes and see her Mama smiling, leaning down to blow the wild wishes into the air.

In the solitude of the phone booth, Maggie cried for Janie, but there would never be a time in her life when her tears weren't also mixed with tears for their Mama.

Maggie knew if it were her, Janie would be on her way to see her no matter what she said. Janie would be there, by her side. Janie wouldn't have left in the first place.

13

Janie never felt so close to Jesus as she did during those weeks when she stayed on with the sisters. There were three of them, all girls from poor towns spread out across the state, showing up so desperate and sad, carrying the burden of both a life and a secret story, sagging with shame. But those sisters made them strong again. They didn't see the shame, they saw life. Perhaps even more importantly, they saw rebirth and resurrection in the faces of those downtrodden girls. They were determined to hold them in the light, to release them back into the world stronger and more true of faith.

The sisters' home was down a long country road on the edge of the woods. There were no men nearby. Sister Rosemary and Sister Teresa ran the home with clockwork precision. Each morning they woke the girls at dawn. Sister Rosemary would take them out for a long walk in the early morning light. She knew so much about the woods, exclaiming with delight over sightings of a wild turkey, or the careful tracks of a buck. She knew the names of all of the trees and flowers, mountain laurel, hemlock, twisted fern. Sometimes she would stop and grab tightly to the hand of whoever was closest to her to point out what she saw to be a particularly beautiful patch of moss.

"That's God's work girls—right there!" she would exclaim. Sister

Rosemary had a deep scar on her right cheek, shaped like a crescent moon. When she smiled or laughed, it transformed into a dimple of sorts, making her appear even more delighted. Their walk always ended at the garden outside the house where they gathered what was left of the green tomatoes as fall progressed.

Sister Teresa was quiet, but equally kind, serenely joyful. Whereas Sister Rosemary shined outside in the woods or with her hands deep in the garden, Sister Teresa came alive in the kitchen. Sister Rosemary would venture out with an ancient looking shotgun, bringing home to Sister Teresa rabbits, squirrels, an occasional pheasant. There were stews and pot-pies and soups and biscuits. But what Janie would come to remember most was how Sister Teresa transformed those unripe, green tomatoes. She would serve plates of them fried and burned around the edges, with a speckled, creamy white gravy on top. Janie found herself waking up thinking about them each morning.

The sisters asked no questions of the girls' past. They delighted in their growing bellies, asking about their babies' movement. At first the girl's were shy; they had spent so long hiding their "condition" that to have someone ask about the life inside took some getting used to, but eventually they relaxed. Janie was the most far along. Emily, fourteen, looked like a little girl playing dress up, with a pillow shoved underneath her shirt. Sometimes she would sit and stare at her growing belly, like she was still trying to figure out how it got there. Ruth was seventeen and reminded Janie of her Maggie. She took to going out hunting with Sister Rosemary and had to be begged to take a rest in the afternoon, to put her feet up. She showed no signs of fear, only unconfined desire to get past this colossal mistake she had made.

The girls were not to attend church, their sinful condition to be hidden from the eyes of the innocent virgins who graced the pews, but every Sunday they prayed and there were hymns. Sister Rosemary played guitar and belted out anthems to the Lord. She sang ballads of all kinds and lullabies too, and whatever other songs the girls requested. They would all end up singing out loud until Sister Rosemary concluded their worship with a resounding, "Alleluia."

At night, there were more prayers and stories, so many magical stories. Sister Rosemary read them *Robin Hood, The Little Match Girl, The Gift of the Magi, The Little Princess*. Janie, warm underneath her thick quilt, had never felt happier.

Christmas came. Sister Rosemary and Sister Teresa had warned them not to expect anything from their families; communication was forbidden by the Church during this time of shame. On Christmas Eve, Sister Rosemary had them bundle up and go outside with her to find a tree. They all decided on a small one on the edge of the woods.

They decorated it that night and feasted yet again, and Sister Teresa passed out cookies. In the morning they each awoke to a package under the tree. Sister Teresa knitted for each one a baby blanket to wrap their babies in before they were given away. "It is full of my prayers," Sister Teresa said quietly as each girl held her blanket, imagining the small life it would someday cover.

"Thank you," was all Janie could manage.

By January, she was enormous and knew her time to be with the sisters was coming to an end. The doctor had come out to visit the girls and told Sister Rosemary that Janie would be ready soon and to head to the hospital when there were signs of labor. Sister Rosemary took to starting the ancient truck out front every morning to make sure it was still running and ready to go for the girls.

One day Sister Rosemary asked Janie to take a walk with her down to the frozen pond. She had hammered out a hole through the ice and was hoping to catch some pickerels for supper. Winter had closed in.

Sister Rosemary chatted about all sorts of things, the weather, the birds still left, what kind of fish they were most likely to find still biting beneath the ice. Finally she stopped.

"Janie, I need your help. You will be the first of the three of you to go and I want you to do something for me, something for the other girls. I want you to be brave when it's your time because when it's their time, that is all that they will remember. I know you will be afraid, but pray for strength until I can get you out the door and into the car. Then I don't care if you scream and cry the whole ride to to the hospital—I'll be there for you. Let the girls see you strong when you walk out that door, so they have something to hold on to, to believe in, your strength."

"I can do that," said Janie.

"I know," said Sister Rosemary. "I know you can."

They got to the pond finally, and scooped off the thin layer of ice that had formed overnight, over the hole through the ice, and attached their still wriggling minnows to their hooks with frozen hands, dropping their lines down into the dark, winter water.

"Sister Rosemary do you mind if I ask you something?" asked Janie.

"Sure, Janie."

"How did you get that scar?"

Sister Rosemary paused long enough to let her fingertips rest gently on the scar itself, quickly returning her hands to the fishing pole.

"Janie, my past is like a deep, dark well. If I lean too far over to look inside I'm liable to fall in and never get out. I wake up each day and start fresh, looking for Jesus. And I find him, I find him everywhere and sometimes in the most unexpected places. I don't know much, but I do know that even out of the deepest darkness there can come light. Even resurrection. I've seen it happen myself."

They ended up catching two good-sized pickerels and a perch. Janie ran her fingers over the perch's symmetrical, orange stripes, blazed across its iridescent scales, before dropping it into the bucket.

They started walking home. Ahead the sun came out, illuminating the frozen branches of the trees lining the path, transforming the ordinary into the brightest of glimmering, winter light.

14

Janie awoke in the middle of the night with a stiffness in her belly. It passed quickly but it was enough to leave her wide awake. In the same room Ruth and Sarah slept silently, bodies turned, arms draped protectively over their bellies, their babies. The stiffness came again later, a sudden, but subtle wave over her skin. The third time Janie knew, knew that this was the day she would bring her baby into this world. Shortly after first light, her water broke, forcing her to get up, and gather the pile of sodden sheets beneath. Sister Rosemary greeted her at the door, hastily taking the wet sheets from her, wrapping her shoulders in a shawl. And then, wordlessly, they were all there, Sister Teresa, Emily, Ruth, all touching her, beginning to whisper words of comfort. Her eyes met Sister Rosemary's who knew at that moment that all Janie wanted to do was collapse into their strong arms and weep, to finally let go and tell them how afraid she was but mostly how sad she was to have to leave. Sister Rosemary nodded her head, and said softly, but firmly, "Janie—you're going to be fine."

Janie let her eyes rest on Rosemary's face, on that scar, wondering for the thousandth time what act of monstrosity would leave such a mark. She took a deep breath and stood tall. Janie clenched each hand that reached her way with a fierceness they had never seen before.

"God bless you all. I know I won't be here, but my prayers will follow you and your baby out this door, too."

"God Bless you, Janie. God bless your baby. We'll be praying for you, every day, you and your baby. God bless you, Janie."

It was all they had, these words uttered into the bitter dawn, the cold turning their prayers into vanishing clouds of white smoke.

Sister Rosemary helped Janie into the passenger seat of the warm pick up and they waved goodbye as they drove down the road. Janie would remember pieces of the trip to the hospital: her forehead pressed against the cool window glass, Sister Rosemary humming an incessant tune, her white knuckles grasping the steering wheel tightly, acutely aware of the icy road ahead.

By the time they arrived at the hospital it was too late for medication, too late to do anything but wheel Janie straight into delivery. The nurses stopped Sister Rosemary at the door. She paused to brush the matted hair off Janie's forehead, and she leaned over and kissed her goodbye. "Be good," was all she said. She pulled out the baby blanket that Sister Teresa had given Janie for Christmas and handed it to the nurse. "This is to wrap up her baby before she goes, be a love and make sure that happens won't you?" The nurse hurriedly agreed.

With Sister Rosemary gone, quickly faded behind a pair of heavy steel doors, Janie at last wanted to cry out, to tell them that this was all wrong. She wanted the doctor to know that this was how her Mama's baby died, that this was how her baby would die, too. The nurse and the doctor looked so calm, they couldn't know that she was in such pain, such danger. The nurse kept telling her what to do, how to breathe, when to push. The pain got worse, more foreign, more emblematic of the terrible end Janie had seen coming all along.

But she was wrong. After one last excruciating wave, they called out, "It's a girl!" They held her up, a writhing ball of life, with eyes that were open for Janie to see. Her baby girl—she was alive. That was the thought that kept calling out in Janie's head. My baby is alive. They swaddled her quickly and Janie was just taking in her small face, her dark hair, when the nurse told her to kiss her and say goodbye, that it would be better to say goodbye now. Janie leaned her face over her daughter's and breathed deeply, trying to take in every last bit of her daughter's scent. She remembered the smell of dirt in the backyard as her Mama dropped seeds into her tiny palm to plant. She remembered the smell of her Mama in the morning when she would crawl into bed beside her at first light. She remembered Maggie's wet hair leaning against her shoulder after swimming in the creek. It was a smell so real, so familiar and addictive in moments. *She is mine. Mine!* thought Janie fiercely as though the word held meaning for the first time. She kissed her baby and silently asked her Mama to keep her safe. They lifted her out of her arms and she was gone.

15

Janie awoke to see her Daddy sitting at the end of her bed. He smiled and pulled his chair closer to her, stopping short of rising up to kiss her cheek.

"How's my Janie?" was all he could muster.

"Not so good, Daddy," said Janie, repeating the now familiar motion of swallowing back tears. Seeing her Daddy brought back her baby's face in even sharper relief. "She was his grandbaby," thought Janie. And then, "She is his grandbaby."

Her Daddy said nothing more, for which she was grateful. He sat there by the edge of her bed for hours while she feigned sleep, sometimes humming, sometimes ever so softly tapping his foot, hat in his hands always.

The night nurse arrived at seven.

"Time to go. Visiting hours are over, sir," she said firmly.

"Thank you," Daddy answered quietly, full of submission.

"Well now Janie, I'll see you tomorrow, sweetheart," he said.

Janie could only shake her head yes, certain that if she broke her silence an endless wail of agony would escape from her lips. She could feel it pressing inside of her, like a wild animal caught in a trap.

Daddy walked to the edge of her bed, but stopped short, nodding slightly to the air above her, unable to come close enough to kiss her cheek.

Something inside her Daddy broke that first time he saw his Janie, hidden in those crisp white hospital sheets, her eyes shut tight to the world. His Janie, a mama so soon, already grieving about her child. He wanted to tell her that it was better this way, that the life of a child here was full of heartbreak, that she was right to let her baby go, but he knew he would be lying. He still saw the face of the baby girl they lost and he'd held her but once. Violet, her name would come to him without warning, a crazy man's whisper disguised as a cough.

Something about his Janie, so bereft, so suddenly foreign to the world of children, spoke to him above all the other heartbreak and bad luck he'd seen in his life. This wasn't the Lord's work and it wasn't even the Devil's, this was his burden and his alone. There were no songs to sing to explain away your fifteen-year-old daughter in a hospital bed giving away her "fatherless" baby. That story matched no tune. He never drank again.

Daddy returned each morning, silently resuming his bedside vigil.

"Good morning, Janie. Can I get you anything, sweetheart?" Daddy would ask, desperate for something he could do, but still Janie could only shake her head no.

Janie noticed how Daddy arrived each day with his hair neatly combed. As she watched his shaking hands, she pictured him alone inside their house in front of the tiny mirror her mother had hung on their bedroom wall, the comb slipping from his grip again and again.

Janie could tell he wasn't drinking, not just by the shaking hands, but by the pallor of his skin, so pale it was almost translucent, revealing the trail of broken veins that climbed across his face, like the map of a warring country.

16

They kept her a whole two weeks, courtesy of the Roman Catholic Church. Janie barely emerged from her bed. She gathered from the rounds of medical residents who followed Dr. Baker into the room that the birth of her baby had been hard on her. She didn't care. She welcomed the blood, the perpetual deep aching, the aftermath of childbirth. It matched her shattered heart.

Her breasts had filled with milk, milk for her baby girl in the days after her delivery. The nurses had brought her warm towels to ease the hard swelling. The swelling had passed, but Janie felt like she could still smell her baby's milk spoiling inside of her.

"Why, Jane, you are a young girl and you are going to be up and back to yourself in no time! I bet you fit back into your old clothes by next month, you lucky girl!" the day nurse exclaimed.

Janie closed her eyes and pushed her head into the pillow.

"You can't fool me—I know you are awake, honey! I peeked my head in here a few minutes ago when you weren't looking and saw you with your eyes wide open looking out that window," she broke into a hum and started to prop up Janie's pillows behind her head.

"Now I bet you can't wait to go home. Don't worry, honey, before you know it everything will be back to normal. You've just gotta be a big girl now, ok? Ok?"

Janie shook her head, praying that this would be enough to send the woman on her way. Dr. Baker walked in while she was still fussing with Janie's sheets.

"Why good morning, Dr. Baker. I was just telling our patient here that she was going to be her old self again soon!"

"Thank you. I'm going to have a talk with her now, too. Her father is waiting in the hall—can you send him in?"

"Of course, Doctor," she smiled again at Janie.

Daddy walked in and came to stand by Janie's side.

Dr. Baker nodded to Daddy as he entered, "Well Jane, we're going to send you home tomorrow. I wanted to tell your father here that you need to take it easy for a few weeks, but that I don't anticipate any problems. You are a young, strong woman. I'm sure this experience has taught you a thing or two... So, do you have any questions for me?"

Janie looked into his eyes and let the litany of questions that had tortured her over the last two weeks pass silently across her mind. *Where did her baby sleep? What did she wear? Did she take to the bottle? Does she suck her thumb? Does she like to sleep on her belly? What does her face look like when you go to pick her up in the middle of the night after she has been crying? Do they pick her up?*

"No. I don't have any questions," she answered.

Dr. Baker stood up.

"Well ok then. I wish you luck," he said and left.

She watched him walk out the door.

"I'll be here first thing tomorrow Janie, to take you home," said Daddy. Janie stared ahead, finally wishing to die, to sleep forever, anything to escape the abyss left by her daughter. She prayed to never see dawn.

17

"I knew your Mama," came the voice. Janie, cringed, expecting it to be another nurse trying to get her to engage. It was morning. She was still alive. It was the woman who cleaned her room, nameless and faceless to Janie until now. Her name tag read, "Alice."

"I knew your Mama," she said again. Janie remained silent.

"I had my baby when I was young, young like you. I brought my baby boy home to live with my Mama. He lived four months and three days. His name is Edward."

Janie looked up. "I'm sorry," she whispered softly.

"When my baby died, people came from all over the Patch to bring us food and to tell us how sorry they were about my little boy. They were good Christians, but the moment they set down a covered dish, or offered their prayers, they backed right down the steps and up the road. People are afraid of grief, even more than polio or scarlet fever, they think it's something you can catch. I know better—there's nothing you can do to outrun grief. But not your mama, your mama didn't run. She brought me a plate of food and she sat right down next to me, didn't ask me nothing, didn't say a word, but she stayed. I will be forever thankful to your Mama for that kindness. I know when she lost her baby she never came back to you, but she was a good soul, your mama."

"Thank you," said Janie, her voice breaking.

Alice came and took her hand. "Honey, I know you want to die. I know you want to give up. I've watched you try to disappear into those sheets. I know you gave your baby girl away, to give her a good life with a good family. But you're still her mother, you will always be that baby girl's mother. You gave her the gift of life and now you can live a proud life for her, too. You are somebody's mother. You can't quit. I carry my baby boy in my heart with me each and every day. For him I carry on because when we are together in the next life I want to take him into my arms with my head held high."

Janie wept quietly.

"Now why don't you let me help you clean yourself up and get ready for your Daddy to take you home?"

18

Daddy arrived later that morning. "Time to go, sweetheart. Time to go home."

As they wheeled Janie down to the exit doors she marveled at the pulsating life of the hospital. She had felt alone in her small world of birth and grief. Once outside, Janie searched the faces of the steady stream of nurses, doctors, patients, and relatives for some kind of recognition, some kind of remorse, but they remained oblivious to her empty arms. As they crossed the threshold and Daddy helped Janie stand up, she looked back one more time. This grey building was the only place she had ever held her baby girl. She wanted to run back inside, to lock herself in her room once more so she could relive that moment over and over again. But even that room wasn't hers anymore. Another mother, another story, would claim its space.

Joseph stood waiting, holding the car door open. His face broke into an effortless smile, "We've missed you, Janie." He bent to hug her but stopped when he saw her face tighten.

"It's ok, just let me help you," he said softly.

He gently helped her into the back seat where there was a white box from the bakery where Maggie used to work, tied up neatly, filling the car with the smell of sticky buns.

"I brought you something—I didn't know what the food would be like in there."

"Thank you, Joseph," Janie thought of Joseph keeping up his routine of visiting the bakery, even with Maggie gone. At that moment, she knew Maggie would never love Joseph, not the way he wanted, and she knew that she had to find a way to get back to the hospital.

Janie remembered the stories she'd heard in Sunday school about pilgrims traveling to Lourdes to the cave where a young peasant girl had seen a vision of the Virgin Mary. When she was little, Janie couldn't believe that thousands and thousands of people would travel all the way across the ocean to France to see the place where some poor girl said that she had seen the Virgin Mary. But now she understood. Even an empty cave and nothing more than the story of a face so briefly present are enough to sustain a dream.

19

Sixty-two days old. Her baby girl was sixty-two days old.

"Can I make you a cup of tea, Daddy?" Janie awoke to find Daddy, sleepless now without the drink, standing downstairs by the window, waiting for dawn.

"Go back to bed, honey. I'm ok."

Janie came and stood by him.

"Getting warmer out isn't it? Can smell spring coming," Daddy said.

Janie winced. She never could tell when, but out of nowhere something would cut her to the quick. Spring. First warm sun, yellow crocuses pushing through in the most unexpected places. Robins. Patches of green grass soft and lush enough to lay a baby on. Life reappearing everywhere. How dare spring come again.

Daddy watched her face.

"I'm going to make us both some tea," he said and shuffled to the kitchen.

Dawn came quickly, the bright light harsh, exposing corners in their small house where dust gathered, forgotten. Janie started to feel the panic rise inside her at the prospect of another day alone.

"I'm going to go down to the hospital today," she announced unexpectedly while Daddy was meticulously rinsing his teacup in the sink.

Daddy put the cup down and looked at her.

"You ok?"

"I'm going to go back there and ask about a job. There. At the hospital."

Janie felt the weight of his stare, his fears. He didn't believe her, assuming she was in some kind of trouble again. She knew that's what he thought. Somehow, a mere sixty-two days later, she was knocked up again, as though she were a drunk like him and all it would it take is one sip to fall back into shame.

"The hospital?" he repeated.

"It's nothing like that, Daddy. I'm fine. It's just that I think I'm ok enough to work again, to find a job. Better than sticking around here doing nothing all day."

"Why don't you want to go back to the priest's house?" Daddy's voice became lower, darker.

"I don't want to..."

He cut her off, "Why not? Why don't you want to go?"

"I just don't want to work there anymore."

"Did something happen there, Janie? Why did you never go back? What happened? Janie, what happened?" he asked more forcefully.

Janie said nothing.

After a moment, Daddy, staring hard, let the words escape, "What did you do?"

Janie stood up, stepping backwards away from him in her rage, her disbelief, "What did I do? What did I do, Daddy? You wouldn't have known anyway! You were so drunk half the time you barely made it home!"

Daddy looked anew at his daughter, utterly transformed from the little girl he remembered. He finally spoke, "I'm just asking..."

"Well stop asking because it's too late! It's too late for you to ask, too late for you to do anything. My baby is gone. I am trying my best to make this right, I am trying to keep on going and no you don't have to worry about me going around with anybody anymore, shaming you anymore because I am done. I am completely and totally done. I am dead inside Daddy. I wake up every day shocked that I am still breathing in this place. I am dead. And so yes, I am going back to the hospital because that is where I had my baby. I had a baby, Daddy. A baby girl that I gave up and who went away and who I will never see again, and who no one ever talks about or asks about as though she never even existed. I am going back there because she did, because the memory of her is the only thing keeping me alive. Not you, not some boy. She is. She is all I've got."

Daddy wanted to take her in his arms. He wanted to tell her how sorry he was. He wanted to ask her what his granddaughter looked like. The words pooled inside of him, scattered, then lost. He said nothing. He gathered his things and headed quickly for the door. He stopped before pushing it open.

"I'm sorry, Janie," he said without turning around.

Janie said nothing.

She took the bus down to the hospital later that afternoon. She lingered out front making sure it was the same building that Sister Rosemary had delivered her to the night of her daughter's birth, the same doors she had walked out of two short months ago.

She was baffled again by its ordinariness, by the pace of life so uninterrupted by her presence. Her breathing daughter had been her vision alone; she would be the sole pilgrim to this site of miracles.

She went in discreetly, wandering the halls until she found a woman pushing a mop bucket out of a patient's room.

"Excuse me, I am looking for Alice."

"Alice?"

"Yes, Alice. I'm sorry I don't remember her last name. She cleans the patients' rooms?"

"I know who she is. Are you family? Is everything ok?"

"Everything is ok, yes. I met her here."

"Ok. She's on the third floor cleaning now. I'll go up and tell her you are here—what's your name?"

"Janie, Janie Coyle. She might not remember me, I just need to ask her a question," Janie's voice became panicked. She felt suddenly foolish, desperate.

"It's ok, I'll get her."

"Thank you."

Janie sat in the lobby waiting for Alice, wondering what she had been thinking, if perhaps she had even imagined the conversation she had with this woman. But then she saw Alice turn the corner. There was not a trace of surprise across her face when she saw Janie waiting.

"Hi, Janie. Good to see you, sweetheart. You look good."

Janie wanted to cry, to fall into the arms of this woman, so grateful was she to be recognized, to be remembered here.

"How can I help you, honey?" Alice asked softly.

"I'm sorry if I'm bothering you. I didn't know how else to find you. I came to see about a job, a cleaning job. A cleaning job here, with you, in this hospital. I've cleaned before—I'm real good at it. I just would like to be able to come back here... to spend some time here—where I had my baby. I know that might seem crazy..."

Alice patted Janie's arm and spoke quietly. "There's nothing crazy about it, Janie. I understand. It's ok, honey. I can talk to somebody. I can ask. I'm sure we could use some more help here. Did you have your lunch yet? I'm about to go have mine. Why don't you come with me?"

20

Janie got the job cleaning with Alice. They took the bus into town to the hospital together each morning. They worked hard, each of them taking pride in entering a room of sickness and sorrow and making it shine.

There were always miners. Young boys with legs rendered useless by falling rock. Old miners finally so full of dust they couldn't walk anymore, counting their final ragged breaths. But the burns were the worst. The stench of human flesh, the wild eyes of miners trying to remember what happened last, when the flames caught them, how they got out, who didn't.

Janie and Alice would linger in these rooms, waiting patiently for the doctors to leave so they could visit with these familiar faces, whispering God loves you and hopeful prayers, promising to carry messages back to the Patch.

At the end of each day, Janie would walk to the room where she'd delivered her baby girl. She would stand briefly outside the door and pray for her daughter's safekeeping, noting the exact number of days since she'd seen her last. Alice, silently respectful of this ritual, would wait for her in the lobby.

In the evenings at home, Janie would put supper together for Daddy and fall gratefully exhausted into bed, having endured another day.

Joseph took to coming by in the evenings and sitting on the porch with them now and then. There was always plenty of Patch gossip to go around, enough to fill the tender space inside each of them that threatened to scream out at any moment.

"Heard much from Maggie lately?" Daddy asked Joseph one night.

Janie could see how the question pained him, how the joy darkened in his face.

"A few letters. They keep them real busy she says. Exams. Working weekends."

"Did she tell you if she was coming home anytime soon?" Daddy asked.

Janie wanted Daddy to stop, knew his questions served a darker purpose.

"No, sir. She didn't say," Joseph answered.

"Can't stay ahead of that girl, Joseph, no sirree. She's gonna do just as she pleases. Just as she pleases," Daddy whistled low.

"I'm sure she'll be home soon. She's been real busy I know," Janie said softly.

"Yeah," Joseph answered, quietly avoiding Janie's eyes.

They sat together for a while in silence until Daddy stood up and announced he was going to bed. Joseph got up to leave, too.

"You don't have to leave on my account. Stay and talk to Janie. I'm sure she'd like the company," Daddy laughed, mockingly.

Janie froze in her rage. Daddy walked inside and Joseph sat back down quietly and said nothing for a while.

"He's probably right, huh Janie? I probably picked the wrong sister to keep company with?" Joseph asked. Janie was silent.

"Janie? He's just an old man worried about his daughters. Janie? You ok?"

Janie looked at Joseph. Even now, having seen his face countless times, she was struck by his beauty. She felt a rush of warmth in the pit of her stomach that she recognized as desire. She reached out and gently touched the side of his cheek. She watched as he ever so slightly recoiled. She dropped her hand.

"I'm sorry. I'm gonna go into bed now. I'm tired," she said softly turning her face away.

"Janie wait! Janie? I'm sorry—I'm sorry about everything—the way everything turned out?"

"I know you are. It's not your fault."

"It's not yours either. I wish everything was different."

Janie kept her head down and walked inside, up to her room and crawled into bed, under the thick quilt. It smelled stale, like her. Hot tears spilled out of the corners of her eyes. The only man that had ever wanted her had been alone and desperate and had wanted her only in secret. Her face, her used up body held no allure. If Joseph had leaned into her hand, ever so slightly, his warm cheek resting in her palm, she would have gone home with him, gone home with her sister's lover. But he didn't want Janie. He wanted Maggie. They always did.

Janie barely slept that night. At dawn she walked downstairs to find Daddy, ever present at the kitchen table. She started to walk back upstairs.

"I was thinking of walking down to church today. Would you come with me?" Daddy asked without looking up. Janie stopped on the stairs.

Janie hadn't been to church since she felt her baby move inside of her. Of all the things Father Timothy had taken from her, that seemed to be the most cruel. Church had become the place where she looked forward to seeing him, finding in even his most distant glances and basic prayers hidden meaning, hidden messages meant for her. It had become his house, not hers.

"We can sit in the back," Daddy went on, "They're all sinners—the whole lot of them—we'll fit right in. They'll get over it, they always do. Will you come with me?" Daddy asked, finally looking at her directly.

"Yeah, I'll come. Just give me a minute to get dressed." Janie answered quietly.

They walked in once the service had already started, quietly finding a place in the back pew. A new priest had arrived, animated and confident, pacing up and down in front of the altar, ignorant of the space Father Timothy had once occupied.

Janie looked to the windows, their stained glass depictions of the stations of the cross. She closed her eyes and sat remembering her baby's face.

When the service was over she tried to make her way quickly to the back of the church, but she was too late to avoid the exiting crowd.

"Janie, good to see you. You look good," called a neighbor.

"Janie, good to see you, hon—are you keeping this crazy fella out of trouble?" a friend of Daddy's from the mine.

"Janie sweetheart, so glad to see you here," a whispered voice and a tight squeeze.

Father Timothy was gone, his baby, their baby girl, while so very alive, still lost to her forever except in prayer. Janie imagined all of the angels that they prayed for collectively suddenly appearing, floating above them, all the men lost in the mine, the babies lost in sickness, the many lives cut short by a dizzying array of misfortune, angels like her mother, all gone. This was still their home.

21

It started late spring, a subtle cough Daddy blamed on the golden rod and ragwort gathering on the hill behind their house. It stayed through summer, through the uncurling of the ferns and the bloom of mountain laurel. By summer's end, Janie knew the cough was here to stay, marking her Daddy's time in the mine, like crow's feet or gray hairs reveal one's age. Still she didn't worry. Miners' cough was everywhere. Old granddaddies sitting on their porches years out of the hole, still lived on with its constant company.

They had a bumper crop of tomatoes that year. That fall Janie prepared dozens of them like Sister Teresa had. Daddy ate them by the plateful. After dinner he would take his plate to the sink and insist on washing the dishes himself, humming a soft tune, sporadically interrupted by his muffled cough. They had made a kind of peace with each other, Daddy and Janie, found kinship in their quiet suffering. She didn't see him dying. She didn't see his frame start to wither. She didn't see him clutching the chair to steady himself when he got up from the table. His cough had become a familiar cadence. She didn't hear its menacing rattle. Her mind was too cluttered already, spilling over with conjured pictures of her baby girl. Janie let her thoughts wander to places that she shouldn't have, places that were hard to come back from, to let go. She imagined her baby girl crawling across their wooden floor. She saw her sitting on Daddy's lap while he sang *Que Sera*, reaching a small finger towards the deep dimple in his chin. She imagined her warm body tucked in next to her at night. She saw her laughing, holding onto Janie's finger, trying to stand. The days were getting colder, winter was coming. Her daughter would turn one this winter. Would she notice the falling leaves, the first snowfall? Would someone carry her to the window to show her the outside? Janie's Daddy was dying, but all she saw was her baby girl, alive, yet out of reach.

Christmas morning they woke and walked to church, Daddy taking Janie's arm firmly. At the time she thought it was so he could guide her, protect her, help her get through what he knew would be another day of longing and sorrow. As they approached the church doors, Daddy stumbled slightly, grabbing fast to Janie to right himself. The church seemed to teem with children, babies crying out, toddlers with runny noses trying to escape down the aisle, frazzled young mothers hushing and scolding, their arms full of babies. Janie pretended to pray but she really just needed to close her eyes.

Maggie didn't come home that Christmas either. She'd been gone a year and a half. That May she was to graduate—a nurse. Like the Christmas before she sent money and small neatly wrapped gifts and letters explaining that nursing students who worked in the hospital during their vacation were paid handsomely. Daddy and Janie opened the letters together silently before bed.

Janie stayed awake deep into Christmas night. She remembered how last Christmas her baby girl was still inside her, hers alone. She had carried her baby with her everywhere. She wished for each moment of her pregnancy back again so she could savor it without fear. The first waves of nausea announcing her life, her daughter's kicks like magical eruptions against the smooth skin of her belly.

After Christmas it was New Year's, a different year than the one in which she had given birth, time marching on, regardless of her suffering. Janie's daughter's first birthday arrived on an uncharacteristically warm winter's day. It was a Sunday. Janie didn't emerge from her room. She could hear Daddy quietly pacing downstairs. She felt grateful knowing that at least he remembered what day it was, otherwise he would have peeked his head in, or called to her.

Alice knocked on their door at eight o'clock.

Daddy let her in.

"Good morning, Mr. Coyle. I'm here to see Janie."

Janie could hear them exchange muffled words. She heard the door close and knew her Daddy had left. She heard Alice put the tea kettle on the stove.

A little while later Alice knocked softly at her bedroom door.

"Janie?"

Janie didn't respond.

"Janie, I'm going to come in now. I brought you some tea."

Janie kept her back to her, ashamed of her tear streaked face. Alice came and sat on the twisted quilt.

"Janie, this day is going to come every year, God willing. On this morning, somewhere your baby girl's adopted parents are waking up and thanking God for her, for you, for your gift. Your sacrifice is their greatest gift, their greatest joy. I'm sure of that. Come on, honey—let's get you dressed and walk down to church and light a candle for your baby girl on her first birthday."

Janie was silent for a while.

"I don't think I can. It's not getting any better. It hurts even more now. I miss her so much. I wake up in the middle of the night in a panic that I will somehow forget what her face looked like, what she smelled like, that somehow I will lose that, too. How can I not have a picture of her? At least something she had held onto once? I have nothing. I want her back, Alice! I understand that I can't have her. I know I did the right thing. But it doesn't help—it doesn't stop me from wanting her with me. How do you do it, Alice? How do you go on when no one seems to remember? How do you keep your baby alive?"

Alice sat quietly for a moment before answering.

"I don't. My baby is dead. I watched him die and he wasn't even in my arms when it happened. The doctors and nurses were crowded over him and I know he was afraid. Every day, when I wake up, I see him dying. Every day. It never gets better. Every day I have to tell myself again that he is dead. Janie, your baby girl is alive somewhere with a good family and honestly I don't know which is more painful, but I know it doesn't matter. We are both mothers who lost our babies."

"Look under my bed," Janie said softly.

Alice crouched down and looked under the bed, pulling out *The Common Sense Guide to Baby and Child Care* by Benjamin Spock, MD. She ran her fingers over the blue cover. *Baby boy blue,* she thought silently.

"I took it from the library," Janie said quietly. "I had to steal it because I couldn't have handled the way the librarian would have looked at me if I tried to check it out myself. I want to learn more about babies, what I would need to know if I were the one taking care of her. I'm not a good reader. It takes me a while to read each part. But it makes me feel better. Like I am taking care of her, too. Is that crazy?"

Alice began to slowly turn the pages. The row of paper dolls, secreted away from Father Timothy's bible spilled out. Alice gently picked them up and handed them to Janie.

"It's not crazy at all, Janie." Each chapter heading brought back her baby Edward's face. She would set herself ablaze a thousands times for the chance to change his diaper one more time, to heat a bottle, to wash out his night clothes in the sink.

Janie sat stroking the yellowed chain of paper dolls.

"What's that?" Alice asked.

Janie continued to look down as she answered.

"I took this. I took this from his bible."

"Who?"

"Father Timothy. Remember him? Young priest who was here for a few months?"

Alice nodded, reaching for Janie's hand, somehow knowing what was coming.

"We... we... He was my baby's father. Please don't ever tell anyone. I never told anyone before. Not Maggie even. I found this in his bible that he used to read, to have with him when he was working on sermons. I know what we did was wrong. I know what he did was wrong. But I kept this. I took this from his bible because it seems to me that a man who would hang onto a row of paper dolls couldn't be all bad? I have to believe that. I have to believe that about my baby's father. So I kept this. And it helps. It helps me believe that there was good in him, too."

Alice nodded, tears quietly falling down her cheeks, still holding fast to Janie's hand.

"Why don't we sit for a while and look at this book together, Janie? We're allowed to be mothers, too. Let's read about what your baby might be doing. You have every right to know."

They sat together turning the pages, Alice reading aloud certain sections. For a brief moment, they were just two mothers, sitting side by side, talking about their babies. Nothing more.

"Are you ready to get dressed? The nine o'clock service is over, I'm sure the church is empty now. Do you want to walk over together?" Alice asked hopefully. Janie nodded yes. She gently placed the paper dolls back in between the pages and closed the book, returning it to its shameful spot under her bed.

Alice moved quickly about the room, finding Janie's things, helping her dress, combing her hair gently as though she were a small child. Alice knew that later this would matter to Janie, it would matter how she looked on this day.

When they came downstairs, Daddy was waiting for them on the porch. He handed Janie some folded bills.

"Light a candle for me too, will you, love? For my granddaughter on her birthday," Janie took the bills and hugged him, her face pressed against his sunken frame.

22

The letter came from Janie in April. Maggie was preparing for her final exams. May sixth she would graduate, a nurse, capable of taking her own job in whatever hospital she chose.

Janie's letter told her in no uncertain terms that she was to come home as soon as she could, that Daddy was sick, very sick, and that she, Janie, needed her, needed her home.

Maggie knew she would have to go this time, that she would have no choice now but to return to the place that she had managed to keep at bay for almost two years. Still, she waited two weeks before she responded to Janie, carrying the letter with her always as penance for her lack of devotion.

Come May, she finished her exams, and took the bus home, skipping her graduation ceremony, the celebrations, the farewells to classmates. She walked the two miles from town to her Daddy's house, head down, hoping to avoid being recognized, to delay the announcement of her arrival back into this place. It was unchanged. Even in the spring air she felt the weight of its isolation.

She climbed the steps to their house and paused briefly, wondering if she should knock. She pushed the door open and there was Janie, sitting at the table alone. She looked up shyly at Maggie at first and then stood and came to hug her. The physical touch of someone else was now unfamiliar to both of them and they both felt the other gently back away.

"I can't believe you are here. It's been so long. Your hair, your hair got so long. I like it..." Janie stumbled.

"You look different too..." Maggie could see Janie cringe then she realized what she was saying.

"Your hair I mean, Janie. You cut yours! It looks so pretty. You're so grown up."

Again she could see Janie tremble at these words.

Daddy emerged from the back room, skin ashen, gaunt.

"There she is—my long, lost daughter finally home! I really must be getting ready to die if she's back!"

"Hi, Daddy," Maggie said.

"Hi, sweetheart," he hugged her and she could feel the hollowness inside of him, his insides already ravaged.

Maggie broke away first. Janie started to talk nervously.

"Is that all you brought with you? That bag? Maggie, that's the same bag you left with! And did you walk all the way here from the station? We would have come to get you—I thought you were gonna call. Are you hungry?"

"I'm ok. Just tired. Should I put my things upstairs?" Maggie asked, suddenly formal, strange.

"Sure, here let me help you," Janie offered.

"It's ok. I've got it. I'll be right back down," Maggie said.

"Ok. I'll make us some tea, " Janie added with forced cheerfulness. Daddy said nothing.

"Great, thank you," Maggie added.

She walked upstairs and placed her bag on her bed, freshly made up, opposite Janie's. For years they had shared the same bed until Maggie started her period and then for some reason she felt like she should sleep alone.

She was surprised anew by the shabbiness of the room, surprised to see the same hole in the window screen covered in cardboard, the same flowered chair by the window with the stuffing escaping the corners. How could it be that after all this time when she returned home her mother's absence still stung, could still grow into a piercing ache? When her Mama was alive her smell was everywhere. She'd left small reminders of beauty throughout their house. Piles of smooth creek rocks collected one summer, a gathering of wildflowers placed in a juice glass, a piece of scrap linen to cover the scratches on their dresser. When she died these talismans lost their power and in time Maggie came to see their room, their house, for what it really was. She headed back downstairs.

Janie had set the table with tea and cookies. She looked up at Maggie expectantly.

"This is great, thank you. I am so hungry."

Maggie looked again at her sister, her baby sister, so changed. She was a woman now. She reminded her so much of Mama, not in her hair, cut short to meet her chin, or in her wide face, still scattered with freckles, but in the invisible heaviness she now carried with her, the burden of this place. Like her Mama, Janie looked tired, broken. In that moment, Maggie promised herself that she would never ask Janie about her baby. Others may look at her sister differently, may talk behind her back, but she would do this for her sister. She would act as though nothing had changed, that she was happy to be here with her now. She would not remind her of her mistake. Maggie took her old place at the table.

"Where's Daddy?" Maggie asked.

"He went back to bed. He gets tired real quickly now."

"He's really still not drinking?"

"Not a drop."

"I can't believe it. Since when?"

"Since... oh I don't know. He just stopped finally."

"Well. What is it that he has? What's the matter with him? Why didn't you say in your letter?"

"It's real bad. Stomach cancer," Janie replied, her eyes brimming with tears.

Maggie waited to feel something—shock, sorrow, fear, but nothing came.

"Nothing they can do," continued Janie. "They opened him up at the hospital and sewed him back up again—they said it's everywhere. The man finally gives up booze and now he's sick every morning anyway. He doesn't complain though—he even kept trying to go to work at the mines until Joseph stepped in—he's been real good to us while you've been gone."

Maggie said nothing.

"He's going to want to see you, Maggie," Janie said.

"I know," she paused. "I want to see him, too, of course I do. It's just been a while."

Daddy never emerged again from his room that night. He stayed awake listening to muffled conversation between his girls.

Maggie slept deeply that night. When she opened her eyes Janie was already awake, getting ready for work. From downstairs came the sound of Daddy vomiting. Janie turned to head downstairs. Maggie got up and stopped her.

"I can go take care of him. You go on and get ready for work."

"Are you sure? You just got home?"

"I know, I know I did."

"Thanks."

Maggie knocked gently and pushed open the door leading into Daddy's room. He was hunched over the edge of his bed getting sick into a stainless steel basin.

"I can take care of this," Daddy answered quickly, turning his head to avoid meeting her eyes.

"It's ok, Daddy."

"I said I can care take of it. Go back to sleep."

"Look, this is what I do all the time," Maggie answered abruptly. She would not baby her father.

"I know, but you don't do it for me all the time and I'm sorry if I'm just getting used to this, too. Just give me a minute, ok?"

Maggie left him alone. When she came back she knocked before opening the door. Daddy was lying down with his eyes closed, perfectly still, the basin full of vomit at the foot of the bed. Maggie picked it up without saying a word and took it outside. When she came back Daddy's eyes were open but he still hadn't sat up. Maggie helped him get to a chair and she stripped his bed. She brought him some clean clothes to put on, turning to face the wall to allow him some privacy, pretending to wipe down the dresser. She knew that soon enough even this act of modesty would have to go. She knew the first to die was pride.

"What are they giving you, Daddy?"

"That there for the pain," said Daddy gesturing to a collection of bottles on the window sill.

"But I don't like taking it. I spent half my life drunk and so I might as well stay clear headed as long as I can."

Maggie helped him back into bed and went and made him some toast. When she took it into him he was already sleeping.

She got to work. She scrubbed the walls and floors, changed the sheets, washed the black grime from the window sills, swept the porch.

When Daddy woke up she got him to eat a little something, and led him out to sit in the sun while she worked on the backyard. The beds her Mama had put down years ago were still there. It was time to turn the soil over and plant again.

"You and Janie are workers, like your Mama. She never could sit still, always peeling a potato, or changing a baby, working back here."

Maggie wasn't used to his conversation, wasn't used to this sober man before her now. He was usually either silently entrenched in post drunk guilt, or still drunk, left to mindless rambling she could choose to ignore. He talked about the weather this past winter, about neighbors she used to know, about the new mine boss. Maggie listened enough to keep him talking. Daddy paused briefly.

"Maggie? You know what I have been wondering lately? What do you remember about your Mama? Before? Before she got sick?"

Maggie looked up, "What did you say, Daddy?"

"Your Mama, Maggie. What do you remember about her?"

Maggie felt like she'd been kicked in the gut. She clenched her fists beneath the dirt to disguise her rage.

"What do I remember? I remember a lot, Daddy."

She hoped he'd let her leave it at that, but he didn't, didn't see her anger, disgust. How dare he? How dare he ask for anything more?

"Maggie? What do you remember?"

Maggie sat and looked at him. When her words finally came, they were venomous.

"I remember her hair. I remember brushing her hair. She'd let me and Janie do it, always telling us how good it felt. We used a pink, plastic brush that would be black with her loose strands by the time we finished. I remember how she used to feed me and Janie potato soup, taking turns putting the spoon into each of our mouths, calling us little fish," Maggie paused, eyes hot with tears.

"I remember you making her cry. I remember that, too. She was my Mama, Daddy—I remember everything. I even remember the name of those goddamn ferns," Maggie said nodding to the clump of lush green ferns lining the rock piles scattered on the side of the house. "Resurrecting ferns, like Jesus, Mama used to say, here in our own backyard. Mama said those ferns seem dead but if they can get some light and moisture then they come alive again. "

Maggie looked him dead in the eye, "Mama never came back though, did she Daddy? Mama? She never came back." Maggie knew her words stung.

"What do you remember, Daddy? What do you remember?" she asked fiercely, head back down, hands still hidden in her Mama's garden.

He knew it wasn't a question.

"I'm sorry, Maggie. Thank you for coming home like this. I know I haven't been a good father. I know I wasn't a good man. I want to talk to you, I need to talk to you about Janie. She's not like you, Maggie. She will never leave this place unless you take her with you and I want her to go. I want her to go. That baby broke her heart. She is a young woman. She could still marry, have another life. Take her down to Philadelphia with you when you go back. Promise me you'll make her do that? If not for me, then do it for your Mama."

"Who said anything about me going back to Philadelphia? I got here last night!"

"I know you're going back, Maggie. Promise me she'll go, too. You can't leave her behind this time."

Daddy didn't wait for an answer, but stood slowly and walked back inside.

23

It took two days for Maggie to go see Joseph. Two days before the loneliness of her home filled her up completely, before she felt it boiling at the base of her throat by day's end, before the familiar desperation set in and forced her to flee, to go quickly out the front door, gasping for air, still hours before dawn, to walk the road to his house, wrapped in only her robe, to quietly push open the back door, to climb the stairs to where he slept. She brushed her fingers gently over his outstretched arm so as not to startle him. He opened his eyes effortlessly, as if he had been waiting.

She had forgotten how much she could want him.

"Maggie. I missed you so much," he said, over and over again as he ran his hands over every part of her body, familiar skin, indentations, that he had imagined incessantly. They made love gently, tenderly.

When it was over, it took but moments for Maggie to remember, to feel regret, the burden of contempt.

Joseph, wide awake, continued to talk.

"I was going to come and see you, but I thought I would give you a few days to catch up with Janie, see your Daddy."

Maggie said nothing for a while, closed her eyes to block the tears that threatened to stream out the corners.

She stood up.

"Where you going?" Joseph asked.

"I better get home. Before they get up. You have to go to work too."

"I don't have to go to work today. I'm one of the mine bosses now—I earned a day off."

"No—go. I have to get home before Janie goes to work. Daddy can't really be alone anymore."

"I'm sorry,"

"It's ok."

He stood up and pulled her to him.

"I love you, Maggie. I'm so glad your back."

"I love you, too," she said softly and left.

Janie was awake when she came in. She looked at her accusingly as Maggie climbed back into bed. Maggie was aware of Joseph's scent, clinging to her still.

"You didn't have to come home. You're a grown woman now—you don't have to sneak out to spend the night with your boyfriend."

"I know that. I came home because of Daddy. And he's not my boyfriend."

"Does he know that? Because I'm pretty sure he doesn't. I'm pretty sure he has been waiting for you all this time."

"I never told him that. And I don't know what's going on. I just wanted to go see him, alone. Without anybody watching."

"Like who? Like me?"

"Anybody. It's not really anybody's business."

"Maybe not, but he doesn't deserve to be jerked around by you. If you don't want to be with him you should tell him. It's the right thing to do."

"How would you know?"

Janie said nothing.

"I'm sorry—I didn't mean anything by that. I just don't know what I'm going to do yet. I wanted to see him—but then once I did I felt like I'd made a mistake—just like always. I'm sorry. "

Janie said nothing.

The sounds of Daddy sick reached them from below. Maggie got up and went downstairs. By the time she came out of Daddy's room, Janie had already left for work.

The days began to blend one into another. Daddy just kept getting worse. The stench of him dying began to settle in their house, like wood smoke. No amount of scrubbing could hide the odor of vomit, shit, the remnants of a body getting ready to leave this world. The laundry line was constantly full of Daddy's shirts, his soiled sheets, worn bedclothes, like flags of surrender blowing in the wind in their backyard. He had become too weak to cover himself up when they came into the room, leaning on them to make it to the toilet, to gather the pants that hung off his waist, revealing his nakedness, the skeletal reminder of the man he once was. When Janie got home from work she would pick up where Maggie left off. Maggie was so grateful to see her come through the door. Her Daddy's presence was disarming; he continued to talk to her, to ask her questions. She resented his trying to get to know her now in the final months of his life.

Maggie continued to go see Joseph in the middle of the night. Sleep would never come to her after they made love. Wide awake, she would watch him, the steady rise and fall of his bare chest. She knew he slept so deeply because there was nowhere else he wanted to be, no desire left untapped. Maggie would gently climb from bed, dress, and walk home alone. She loved the quiet of the Patch at this hour, the blackness of the night disguising the gray disarray of her hometown, the dark sky, clear and deceptively promising.

Maggie took a job as a night nurse a few nights a week at the hospital. She said it was to bring in some extra money, but mostly she was anxious to have another life outside of caring for Daddy.

She loved being back at work, loved the defined hierarchy of the hospital staff, attending doctors, residents, interns, nurses, and finally the cleaning staff like Janie. She would come home at dawn and get Daddy settled as Janie left for work, sleeping a few hours here and there.

Maggie had been working about a month when they sent her up to the post op floor. The attending doctor was impressed by her efficiency and attention to detail. He asked that she be sent upstairs to care for the patients after surgery.

One night, they brought in a boy named Jimmy that Maggie knew from way back, his legs crushed by falling rock after an accidental explosion in the mine. Many of their boys had been hurt.

By the time they got Jimmy out, he'd already lost so much blood. Maggie knew he wasn't going to make it. His face was unchanged from the twelve year old she remembered, riding a bike up and down the Patch road, wreaking havoc. He must have just started in the mines. He was small, probably sent down to the more difficult spaces, his youth only granting him a more dangerous job.

Maggie had left his room and was headed down the hall to look in on another patient when she heard the doctor, furiously questioning a group of nurses gathered in the hall.

"Who is the nurse in charge of the patient in room 302?"

Maggie stopped.

"That's my patient. I'm Nurse Coyle."

"Why was his morphine doubled? I did not write for that."

"He is in a lot of pain, doctor..."

"I am Dr. Lane. I know he is in pain! I did not..."

"Dr. Lane, I know that boy. Do you? I know him..."

He cut her off. Hand pressed to his temple, looking down, his words came out spitting, "You know nothing. You are a nurse and you will follow a doctor's orders; I did not request the patient's morphine be increased to such levels."

"The patient in room 302 is James Brennen. I have known him his whole life. He is going to die. You know it and I know it. I received a verbal order from Dr. Baker who, I believe, is your superior. He doesn't want to see that poor boy suffer. If you have a problem with me following his orders then I suggest you go talk to him."

"We don't always know," he answered, suddenly quiet.

"I know," Maggie said waiting to look him in the eye, but he would not look up, his rage having left in a single rush.

He stayed silent, then turned and walked away.

"Son of a bitch," Maggie said aloud.

He died just as Maggie's shift ended. She helped clean his body so his mother could see him one last time. His face alone remained unblemished. When his mother arrived, Janie came into the room, too. She went and stood by the boy's mother, arm draped across her small shoulders, gently rocking underneath her sobs.

Maggie was eager to leave, telling herself that this woman should have some time alone with her son, that her shift was over. But Janie stayed, stayed throughout his mother's tears, stayed throughout her silence, stayed to be witness to the nurses finally covering his face and telling his mother it was time to take his body down to the morgue. Janie stayed.

24

Maggie was off the next night. Joseph showed up at their door around seven, freshly showered, radiating warmth, desire. He leaned in to kiss Maggie.

"Come on. Come with me. Let's go get a drink." Janie came down from upstairs. "Janie you, too."

"But what about Daddy?" Janie asked.

"I'll ask Mrs. Murphy to come look in on your Dad. She can't say no to me," Joseph smiled, leaning in close. "Come on—come out with me."

"I don't know. I'm kind of tired."

"Come on. Please. I want to take you out."

"Janie, what do you say?" Maggie called to Janie in the kitchen.

"You go ahead, Maggie."

"I'm not going unless you are."

"Come on, girls. Just a few drinks. Please."

Daddy's voice came from the back room.

"Go on! Get out of here and let me have some peace and quiet! I'm not gonna die tonight. Go have a good time."

"Thank you, Mr. Coyle! I'll make sure they get home ok."

"All right then. Just give us a minute to freshen up."

The bar was even more crowded than usual that night in the wake of the mine accident. The ones who got out unscathed were feeling lucky, briefly invincible, eager to get drunk. Maggie and Janie settled in at the bar while Joseph made the rounds. A group of nurses they knew from the hospital came and joined them. They laughed easily with Maggie, offering polite questions to Janie. As they got drunker, they ignored her completely. Joseph came and stood at her side. Janie could feel him looking at Maggie, feel the urgency of his proximity to her sister.

"I think I'm gonna go," Janie said abruptly.

"Really? Come on! We haven't been out in ages—relax, have some fun. Please? There is no reason to go home," Maggie answered, annoyed.

"I'm going," Janie answered. Maggie could tell there would be no arguing.

Joseph stepped in, "I'll take you home. I'll take her home, Maggie."

"You don't have to do that. I can get home fine," Janie said.

"No—I'm tired, too. I've got to get up early tomorrow and from the looks of everyone here I'll be the only one actually able to work! Maggie, you stay. Have fun with the girls." He smiled and leaned in and kissed her, pressing money into her fist, "It's good to see you having a good time," he whispered. "Come see me tonight. Later ok?"

Maggie nodded, smiling. She watched as he helped Janie with her coat and they walked out the door.

A little while later a drink arrived for Maggie. The bartender handed it to her and said, "This is from the gentleman at the end of the bar. He'd like to apologize."

Maggie looked down to see the doctor who had argued with her about the patient's morphine sitting alone at the end of the bar. In her rage that day she hadn't looked closely at his face. He was staring at her now, unflinching. There was nothing reminiscent of anyone she had ever met in the contours of his cheeks, the set of his jaw. He was not from around here she knew at once, not one of her people.

She felt her cheeks flush. She raised her glass in thanks and quickly looked away.

Sharon, a nurse who worked with Maggie, watched the exchange, "He's kind of strange, don't you think? Dr. William Lane. Doesn't really say much."

"Where did he come from?" asked Maggie.

"He's from Philadelphia... some rich family."

"Really? Why is he here then? Nowhere else will take him?" Maggie asked, forcing a laugh.

"No—I heard the doctors say he's the best resident they ever had, seems to know even more than they do. Boy genius they say. He is here to practice—more chances for residents to do surgery here I guess than in the big city hospitals."

Maggie took another quick glance down the bar. His eyes had not left her.

"Is he staying here?" she asked quickly, casually.

"Of course not. He was already promised a position at Pennsylvania Hospital. He's leaving here at the end of summer."

Maggie looked again to the end of the bar where he was sitting. This time she let her eyes meet his. She was the first to look away.

The night wore on. There was a contagious air of abandon. Maggie, for the first time in her life, felt the urge to drink too much. There were toasts and stories and laughter and songs, so many songs, the familiar words flowing easily. Suddenly a voice in the crowd shouted, "Doctor! Sing something for us!"

Maggie sat motionless and watched as he slowly stood up, shocked that this stranger was recognized here, called to sing. He had done this before. He raised his glass, took a sip, and looked her way one more time. He walked to the head of the bar and without ceremony or introduction began to sing. There came a hush over the crowd. There was no chorus for them to join, no familiar lines for them to echo. He might as well have been singing in a foreign tongue. It was not one of their songs. But that night it brought the drunken room to a standstill, his solitary voice somehow releasing their collective sadness. When he was finished he sat down and the hush gave way to applause, allowing for a small moment of silence, while he still held them transfixed. Maggie felt her whole body tremble with an unfamiliar desire.

She boldly walked over to where he sat looking down into the half empty glass. "Thank you for the drink. You have a beautiful voice," she said quickly, wanting to owe him no more, but unable to move.

"Please stay. Please sit a while and stay," he asked, never looking up. She paused, still not sitting.

He continued softly, "I don't want you to think I am unkind, that I was being unkind to that patient. I learned a long time ago that I have to force myself to treat each case purely medically, otherwise I don't always trust my decisions. I know I am a very good surgeon, but sometimes I'm not so sure I'm a good doctor, when it comes to talking to the patients, their families. I always think I say too much or too little."

He continued to drink his beer without looking at her. Maggie was startled by this stranger's confession. She sat down next to him, his proximity alone making the back of her neck tingle.

One by one her girlfriends left. Joseph's friends staggered out as well, those still sober enough glared down at her at the end of the bar. She declined their offers of a ride home.

His name was William Lane. He told her about his mother, a woman everyone called Kitty, who ran a theater in the backyard of their home in Philadelphia. He would return there in the fall to take a surgical position at a hospital in the city. He was eager to get back. His father, a doctor too, had died right after William had finished medical school—his heart. He'd always wanted to be a doctor—like his father before him. He asked her what she liked about being a nurse. He asked her about her family, about growing up in the Patch, if she planned to stay.

She awoke in his bed. He was sitting on the edge, fully dressed, gently pushing her hair away from her face, letting his hand run down her chest, trailing his fingers across the side of her hips, as though her nakedness was completely familiar. He brushed his lips across her collarbone.

"I've got to get to the hospital. I left you some tea here."

Maggie blushed, waiting to feel ashamed, disgusted, the familiar regret that washed over her after a night with Joseph, but instead she reached up and pulled him towards her.

The old woman who ran the boarding house where William lived surely recognized Maggie as she rushed out the door. Her glare said as much. Maggie walked back home, through the Patch, knowing that the news would have reached them by now, would have reached Joseph. She felt relieved that they would finally all know the truth. She was not a good person. She was here because she had to be, she wanted nothing more than to never see this place or any of them again. She was deserving of their scorn, their disapproval, their contempt.

Joseph was waiting on the front porch.

She would not lie. At the very least, she would not lie. She stood motionless in front of him and waited. She was conscious of another man's odor permeating her skin, announcing her betrayal.

"Long night?" he asked without looking up.

"I'm sorry."

He began quietly, still unable to look at her, "I didn't believe it when I heard. I had to come here and ask Janie, ask her if you came home last night. I knew she wouldn't lie to me. I knew she couldn't lie. Your sister is too good for that... "

Maggie said nothing.

"It's true then? You went home with that man?" His voice broke.

Maggie nodded.

Joseph continued to speak to the ground, "I can't believe you did this to me. After all this time, after how I waited—all of our plans, all gone in one night... I can't take you back, Maggie. Do you understand that? Do you know what a fool I look like?"

"I never had any plans," she answered coldly, detached.

He looked up, "How can you say that? I've been with you since you were sixteen. I believed I was the only one who was with you. All that time you were gone I waited... I waited for you. I never went home with anyone..."

"I never asked you to wait..."

He cut her off, "You never told me not to! You let me think..."

He quieted his voice again, desperately trying one last time to rescue her, to rescue himself, to find someone to blame. "Did you have too much to drink?" he asked. He added quietly, "Are you sorry?"

She looked at him. He had such a beautiful face.

"I knew just what I was doing."

She watched his eyes, watched him give in to the hatred that had been lurking there all along, disguised as longing, disguised as love. The transformation took but moments.

"You're a whore. Nothing better than a whore."

She watched him walk away, remaining silent and motionless.

25

By sundown they all knew. Their anger was intensified by the fact that Maggie had rejected, humiliated, the best of them, Joseph. She had chosen sides, again. Even Daddy as his new gentle, sober self, stared at her darkly, saying, "Joseph is a good man."

Janie said nothing.

Maggie returned to work as usual, ignoring the sudden coolness of the other nurses. She would catch glimpses of William throughout the day. He found her whenever her shift was ending, pulling her into a fast embrace, whispering plans for when they would meet later, openly telling her of his love, his desire.

She didn't know any better, she would tell herself later. She had thought this was love, as each day bled into the next, when all she could think about was when she could see him again, even when she'd spent a whole night by his side. She didn't question why this man, this stranger, loved her so quickly, so completely, so desperately. Like countless lovers before her, she believed their passion was unique, inexplicable to others.

At night, after she and William made love she would wait for the insomnia to appear that followed her every time she was in bed with Joseph. Instead she would sleep deeply, suddenly, and without dreams. He would have to wake her so she could get home in time to look after Daddy.

"Maggie Coyle—wait and see. She'll be knocked up soon. That rich doctor will leave her as soon as his time here ends. Poor Joseph, she'll be begging him to take her back." The townspeople rallied together in their defense of Joseph. The talk quickly reached Maggie, and Janie too.

But William didn't leave, didn't tire of her at all. They had been together barely a month when he asked.

"I want you to come with me to Philadelphia. I want to marry you."

Maggie laughed at the craziness of his words.

Even in the dark she could tell he was wounded.

"I know I haven't known you for that long, but I feel that in life there are few times when you are absolutely sure. I'm sure. I want you to come with me. I wrote and told my mother all about you. I want to marry you," he could not disguise the urgency in his voice.

"Yes," she answered softly. It had been so easy to say.

"What?"

"I'll marry you."

They woke up the next morning and dressed quietly, each waiting for one to call the other's bluff. William could feel the panic rising in his chest as Maggie moved about silently. Finally she spoke.

"I guess you need to talk to my Daddy? About us? Getting married? And I need to talk to Janie."

He breathed at last, "I'll go today."

26

William arrived at the house later that afternoon. He knocked at the door and Maggie led him inside to where Daddy was waiting. He did not try to stand up to greet William. Maggie registered the shock on William's face as he took in the small room, the windows grey with soot, the single table, the kitchen lined with bottles of pills, Daddy propped up in a chair in the far corner, fly paper dangling above him like a left behind decoration.

Janie came downstairs and said hello, torn between offering William some tea and her loyalty to Daddy. Daddy did not offer him a chair.

"Maggie, Janie, I'd like to talk to this man alone. Please wait outside."

"Daddy… I think…" Maggie began, but Janie took her arm and led her out.

Once they were alone, William started to talk at once, anxiously, his brow glistening with sweat.

"I would like to ask your permission to marry…"

Daddy cut him off, "I know why you're here. Funny you didn't ask my permission to sleep with her did you?"

William was momentarily silenced. He had not anticipated this shell of a man before him now, by Maggie's own words a lifelong

drunk, now left an invalid, to do anything but offer his joyful, relieved blessing.

"I'm sorry—I am sorry if I did anything to offend you, but I do
want to marry your daughter. I want to marry Maggie. I know it's
fast, but I am leaving soon. I want her to come with me, come to
Philadelphia. I've told my family, my mother, about her, and she is
looking forward to meeting her, to welcoming her into our family,
sir."

"Well, seeing as you're a doctor, you probably know that I won't
be much longer of this world, so I won't interfere with your plans."

"I didn't..."

Daddy put up his hand. William fell silent.

"Now listen, for all I know you're a son of a bitch and my younger self would have put my fist through that silver tipped throat of
yours as soon as you walked through the door. But I know Maggie
is going with you—there is nothing stopping that girl. Nothing ever
has—you should know that. But I need to ask you something."
Daddy began to cough. William handed him a tissue, his mono-
gram stitched neatly on the side. Daddy brushed it away.

"You see I'm not worried about Maggie. I know she is going to
be just fine. But I worry about her sister Janie. You might know
her already from the hospital. She cleans the rooms there. She is a
good girl and she's had a tough time. I don't know you from Adam,
but Maggie has taken up with you and I understand you are from a
family of some means... Janie is going to need someone to look out
for her..." his voice cracked unexpectedly and he could feel the tears
fill his eyes. He covered his mouth to cough.

"I apologize. The medicine gets in my head sometimes, I think.
Foolish old man..."

"It's ok, I understand..."

"I don't think you do. She is a good girl, Janie. She never did
anything to harm anyone in this world. She deserves better than
what she's got. Like I said, I don't know you from Adam, but I have
no choice but to believe in your decency, to ask you if you will look

after Janie, too. Take her with you when you and Maggie go down to Philadelphia. She won't be any trouble. Like I said, she's a good girl, but she needs somebody to look out for her."

William shook his head yes, eager to make things right this time. "I understand, I really do. I promise I will take care of Janie, too. I promise I will make her feel welcome always in my home."

"God willing you and Maggie will have children someday and maybe then..." Daddy stumbled over his words again. "I'm sorry. I never thought I would be a man who was asking a stranger to look after his children. Thank you."

"You have my word."

"Good. Now I will do my best to die by Labor Day. You can go on out—tell Maggie I gave you my blessing. Not that she needed it," William stood awkwardly and leaned forward to shake Daddy's hand.

Maggie was waiting outside with Janie.

"How did it go?"

"He said ok... he said we have his blessing. We can talk about it later... It will all work out." William leaned in to kiss her and left quickly.

27

He drove away from Maggie's house slightly shaken. *It is still all ok,* he thought, *It is still perfect.* He had found Maggie. She was the one he needed. He knew it the very first time he saw her, knew when he saw the rage in her eyes as he challenged her that day in the hospital. She never once doubted her choice. And yes, of course he would welcome her sister Janie, would give her a home, too. This time he would do what was right.

William didn't like to ride in the car, especially alone, with no other voices to fill the emptiness. His mind wandered too easily, to other times, other car rides.

They sent him away to school when he was eight. Sent him away from the theater in his backyard, where his mother, Kitty, would sit for hours and tell him stories on the empty stage. Sent him away from the gardens behind the large stone wall where he played hide and seek with Sarah, his mother's maid, who he secretly thought was somehow his other mother, firmly believing that the patch of freckles across her face mirrored his own exactly.

Sent him away from his father, a man he barely knew, a man who changed everything the moment he walked into a room. He could remember Sarah and his mother beginning to talk excitedly, unnaturally, whenever his father appeared, remembered being whisked out back to the theater, far from the main house whenever his Daddy's voice began to interject, to rise.

His father was often gone.

"He is a doctor, a brilliant surgeon, the best. They say he can fix anyone," Sarah told him once, his prolonged absences always explained by his work, others' needs. William never wondered why no one ever came to see them at the house, no one except the gardener occasionally, to help out.

One day as he was running in the backyard, William fell and cut his knee badly on a jagged rock. He sat crying, terrified by the glistening fat revealed beneath the gash in his tender skin. He looked up and saw his father, in a bathrobe, walking towards him up the path. William hadn't even known he was home. He came and sat down on the ground next to William, an act so startling in and of itself that William's tears stopped immediately. He had never felt his father this close to him before. He stared as the blood crept down his son's leg.

"I am so sorry, little boy. I don't know how to help you. I don't even know how to help myself," he said, staring desperately into William's identical eyes.

"But you're a doctor. Sarah said you can fix anything," William answered.

"I know nothing, I know nothing," he said shaking.

And then there was Sarah's face, running, running up the path. He would realize only later that the terror in her eyes had nothing to do with the blood still pouring down his leg. Later, he would understand that his father's agile fingers were already rendered useless by the madness that invaded his head, his heart, a madness that his mother and Sarah tried so desperately to disguise.

"Daddy is a doctor, he can help," he said to Sarah as she took him into her arms while his father sat motionless, tears beginning to form in the corners of his vacant eyes.

"Your daddy is busy, he doesn't have his supplies here, we need to go to the children's doctor, your Daddy isn't a children's doctor, he takes care of grown ups…" she said quickly as he fought against her.

"My daddy can fix this..." he repeated eager to be close to his father again.

His mother appeared to lead his father back into the house. His Daddy never looked back.

He would need fourteen stitches. The scar reminded him of the river Nile.

It was shortly after this time that William's bags were packed. Sarah and his mother climbed into the back of a hired car with him and drove six straight hours to his new school. He listened to his mother and Sarah tell stories and sing songs, filling every possible moment with their voices until they finally arrived. Once he saw his room, the empty bed, the chest of drawers waiting, Sarah beginning to unpack his things, the fear pulsing in his mother's eyes, he realized that they would leave him behind.

"You mean you are leaving? You are leaving me here?" William began to ask desperately, clutching first at his mother's hands and then Sarah's.

"It is such a wonderful school, sweetheart, you are going to like it so much," his mother recited. But even she was unable to make this tale believable.

"Don't leave!" he began to cry, to scream to go home, and a very important looking man appeared to usher his mother and Sarah out and they were gone.

He had never spent much time in the company of children his age. He had lived his life safe, happy, behind the stonewalls of their home with Sarah and Kitty, ever vigilant. He was to learn quickly that the cruelty he'd only read about in fairy tales was real, and often cloaked inside the body of a beautiful young boy whose parents summered in Maine, who ran effortlessly, winning every game, his hair somehow commanding the wind which way to blow.

He stayed at school until he graduated, coming home for Christmas and Easter, spending the last few days of each vacation physically sick with the dread of returning. The first few years he would cry the whole way there until he slept from exhaustion, his mother's face white with panic, her pale hand clenched fiercely by Sarah's brown hand.

When he was old enough to understand the pain in her face, he stopped crying, but his chest still tightened whenever he approached a car door.

He read almost every book in the school's immense library. It was the only way he survived. By junior year one of the beautiful boys had learned the truth, drunk with the excitement of revealing such news.

"My father knows your father. He says he's as crazy as a loon. Do you take after your Daddy?"

In the stories he'd learned by heart the hero always conquered evil. He waited for his day to come, life was long.

After school he'd gone on to college, graduating in three years, then straight to medical school in Philadelphia, grateful to be near home at last, but his mother got him an apartment right near the school rather than have him stay in his old room.

"You will be able to rest more, have more quiet to study..." she told him without meeting his eyes.

He would go home every Sunday for dinner. His father would sometimes be there, more silent than not, the same medical journal propped on his lap each week, the pages unturned.

William was a brilliant student. He wanted to be a surgeon, like his father. He loved the study of the human body, how it worked so beautifully, how the anatomy made perfect, divine sense.

His father came to his graduation. Sarah standing on one side of him and curiously, the gardener firmly on the other.

The news came the very next day. His father was dead. His mother told him to wait, to not come home until the next day. It would not be until years later that he would realize that she had needed time, time to clean up the blood his father had left behind.

When he came to see her, her face had never looked younger, more alive.

Once they heard what happened, the older doctors took William under their wing, shaking their heads at the loss of his father, politely silent about how he died. They helped steer William towards the best positions, recommended that he travel upstate, to the hospital closest to the coal mines, where the brutality of the frequent accidents provided such interesting surgeries. He went, he did what he was told. He did everything he was told. He would be a great surgeon, he would make the right choices, he would, always, do what he was told. But still, there remained moments of indecision, moments where he felt utterly lost, mapless.

One night he walked into a room where a patient had died. They had done everything right, but the body had not responded. William wanted to make one last exacting note in the chart. When he walked in the cleaning woman was sitting next to the patient's bed, holding his lifeless hand. She looked up startled, afraid.

"We are all done in here. You can go," said William.

"I'm sorry, Doctor," she answered nervously, "but you see no one came to see this boy and so I thought I would sit with him for a while, if that's ok. Please."

"He's dead."

She said nothing for a moment, letting her eyes linger on the young boy's face. *He could be sleeping,* she thought. She spoke again.

"I know, I know he is dead. It's just that sometimes, I mean—I sometimes wonder when the soul really leaves the body? I would like to think someone was with him while he made this journey. I know that might sound foolish, but this boy has no family here. Would you mind? Doctor?"

William looked for the first time at the patient's face. A young boy, another young boy he couldn't fix. He felt himself begin to shudder.

"Do you mind if I stay for a minute, too?" he asked quietly.

The woman looked up in surprise, "Of course not."

William took a seat in the chair by the wall. They were silent for a while. "My name is Alice," she offered.

They sat together until they came to take away the boy's body.

William stayed motionless but Alice rose to help them, to gently lift the body, covering the boy's face carefully, as though protecting him from the cold.

William wondered where his father's soul wandered, whether he would ever find rest.

28

Daddy was gone in two weeks time, adding fire to the fading gossip that his oldest girl had gone and shamed him, broken his heart. He'd stayed in bed all that weekend and through Monday, refusing the food Maggie brought to him, silent whenever she approached. She was grateful to leave for her shift that night, grateful to leave the sullen old man with Janie.

When Maggie came home that morning Daddy was already gone. Janie had washed his body and hung the neatly pressed suit he was to be laid to rest in on the door. She sat by his bed crying softly, wearing his ancient tattered sweater wrapped tightly around her small frame.

Maggie stayed put, leaning into the door frame, staring at the stillness of her father.

"Maggie, he said to tell you that he loved you," Janie said hopefully.

Maggie knew she was lying.

Maggie walked down to get the funeral director while Janie stayed with Daddy. She kept her head down so as to avoid conversation. She wasn't ready yet to pretend to grieve. Her face was flushed, her mind remembering the Daddy that never came home, the one that lay drunk, crumpled on the kitchen floor while their Mama, pregnant, strained to pick him up.

The undertaker offered to drive her back while he came to collect the body. Daddy and Janie had worked out all the arrangements when Daddy found out how sick he was.

When they got back to the house, they found Janie still with Daddy. Maggie came and led her out of the bedroom while the men carried Daddy's body to the car. Janie followed them outside, watching as their car disappeared into the distance. In moments, the neighbors emerged, gathering around Janie. She wept openly, receiving their hugs, their tissues, their words of comfort. Maggie watched alone from behind the glass. After a while, she went and started to strip Daddy's bed.

29

The funeral was full of song, hymns that Daddy and Janie had picked out together, hymns about salvation, resurrection, Jesus' guiding light. They drove in the funeral director's car out to the graveyard where they lowered Daddy's coffin into an open grave next to their Mamma's. Daddy had finally seen to picking her out a headstone once he knew he, too, was going to the great beyond.

Her mother's name, etched so clearly into the clean stone, was like the emergence of a ghost. Maggie caught her breath and held tight to William's hand. He had come to stand beside her despite the hateful looks of the crowd. When she began to cry, her tears were for her Mama, whose gravesite Daddy never even once brought them to visit. The name of their baby sister Violet was absent, her lifeless visit into this world unmarked.

Back at the house, alone at last with Janie, Maggie finally spoke up.

"Janie…William is finishing up here at the end of the month. He wants me to leave when he leaves. He wants me to go and live with his mother. We are going to get married—right away. I want you to come with us, come with us to live in Philadelphia. William wants you to come too—in fact he insists on you coming with us. He's already talked to his mother and she couldn't be happier. She lives in a big house there and she said she can't wait to fill it up. She has been lonely without him."

Janie was silent.

"I know you're sad about Daddy, Janie, but we can't stay here anymore."

When Janie finally spoke, the words came slowly, deliberately. "Maggie, I can't leave here, I can't leave, I can't leave my job."

"Janie, you're going to have to leave anyway. We've only been able to stay in this house this long because of Joseph. They will be wanting it for another miner and his family. And your job—Janie you don't need to keep that job."

"I wish I could, I appreciate the offer, please tell William I said thank you, but I can't, I need to be here." Janie's eyes were wild, desperate, pleading with Maggie to understand.

Maggie couldn't hold back any longer. "Janie there is nothing for you here. Nothing in this place for you. You've got to get out of here."

Janie looked at her sister, hating her for the first time. But within that small moment of hate, she remembered. Maggie didn't know. She didn't know that each day revolved around a silent vigil for her daughter, each week filled with pilgrimages to the only place she had ever held her daughter as her own. Maggie knew nothing.

"I can't leave. I'm sorry." There was silence.

When Maggie spoke again, her voice was shaking. "Janie, I didn't want to have to ask you like this, I wanted you to want to come, but there is something else. I'm going to have a baby, William's baby."

Maggie looked down and continued to speak quietly. "I haven't told William this, he is so thrilled that I'm going to have a baby, that we are going to be a family. I haven't told him about what happened to Mama. I'm scared. I'm scared it might happen to me, too. Every time I think of having a baby I think about Mama. I think about how that baby died inside of her and how Mama died too that day. I see our baby sister's face every time I try and picture my baby. I see her dead. And I see Mama... her eyes changed that day—that's what I remember—almost like they turned a different color. Do you remember that? She never looked the same again... I don't want that to happen to me—I won't let it happen. Please come with me, Janie. I don't know anything about William's mother except what he has told me, and what son doesn't love his mother? Please, Janie. Please come with me."

Janie had never seen her sister afraid. She thought of the excruciating hours spent bringing her daughter into this world, a daughter she believed would be born dead, too. She looked at Maggie, at her flat stomach concealing a life inside. A baby. She understood that all of Maggie's dreams of babies were of Mama's baby, of her baby sister's lifeless face against Mama's chest. They had been her dreams too—before, before Janie could close her eyes and see her own daughter, so very alive. Janie looked out the window as a female cardinal rested lightly on a branch on the tree outside. Against the grey, near dusk sky, the bird's colors, usually plain next to its red, vibrant, male partner, seemed aglow. Janie had given up her baby, Maggie would not lose hers. Janie understood her sacrifice to be sufficient for both of them. She knew, with a certainty that she could not explain, that her sister's babies would be safe. No harm would come to this child. It would be safe and adored, like Maggie.

"Your baby is fine. I know it. I'll come with you. I can't stay, but I'll be with you when your baby is born. It's gonna be ok, Maggie. I know."

30

They spent the next few weeks preparing to leave, cleaning out the house, and packing what little they owned. With their Daddy gone, the sisters felt free to look in every drawer, every closet, searching for some part of their past they might have missed. Maggie found nothing worth taking except for a small photograph of her mother the day she married. She looked no older than fourteen, eyes bright and looking ahead in the distance, her long, black hair pulled back from her beautiful face.

Janie found more. She carefully swaddled her secret book about babies in Daddy's old sweater, placing it at the bottom of her bag. She took a moment to look again at the chain of paper dolls, before folding them carefully and placing them again between the thick pages. The dish towels that their mother had made complete with needlepoint purple flowers, the blackened soup pot that their mother said was her own mother's, the quilt that had covered their parents' bed, a bible and a hymnal, and at the last minute, a clump of Lily of the Valley plants, dug up from their backyard, hastily packed into a chipped, yellow teapot. Janie could see her mother leaning over their tiny blooms, taking in their intoxicating smell. *Come here, girls—bend down and get close to the tiny flower—smells like heaven.*

William arrived to pick them up in a borrowed car. He gently loaded in their pile of possessions, taking care with each one, barely containing his own joy.

They drove the two hours to Philadelphia without stopping. Janie was mostly silent, staring out the window as the scenery changed, passing each town, wondering if her little girl had somehow found a home along this path. After a while she pretended to sleep while she allowed herself the luxury of imagining her daughter in her own bedroom, her dark hair almost reaching her chin by now, dressed in a light blue dress, walking across the room, laughing.

William and Maggie allowed Janie her silence, their hands always touching, their bodies desperate to be together again.

They reached William's mother's house by nightfall, a large grey stone home, set back from the street. William's mother, Kitty, must have been looking out the window. She flew out the door the moment they turned down the driveway. She didn't even allow William to fully get out of the car before she wrapped him in her arms, kissing him. She was beautifully dressed, her silver haired pinned up with a jeweled clasp, as though for a formal party. Maggie felt her whole body stiffen. She slowly got out of the car. Before she had time to even be introduced, William's mother had taken her into her arms too, pushing back her hair, finally releasing her repeating, "Beautiful, just beautiful!"

Janie remained in the back seat of the car, looking out the window, utterly bewildered, still clutching the teapot of Lilies of the Valley.

Kitty finally came around to her side of the car and leaned in the window. "Now you must be Janie! Let me help you out of this hot car. Lilies of the Valley! How wonderful! Something from your garden at home? I can help you find a spot for those tomorrow. Now come on in. I am so happy you are finally here! Leave it, leave it—we'll help you get everything else out later. Come inside! Come in!" Maggie and Janie remained speechless.

Kitty draped her arm across Janie's shoulders and led her into the house.

"Sarah, they're here!" William's mother called.

A tall, regal older black woman entered the room. Maggie and Janie exchanged quick glances. *A maid,* Maggie thought in disbelief, *they've got a maid?* And yet Sarah was dressed beautifully, dramatically, her hair too adorned in a matching jeweled clip, not at all how Maggie imagined a maid to look.

Sarah wrapped William in her arms, too. They were about the same height. William leaned into her and Janie noticed that he closed his eyes, as though at last unburdened.

"Maggie and Janie, this is Sarah," William said softly.

"Nice to meet you," Maggie and Janie answered awkwardly, in unison.

Sarah turned to look at both of them for the first time. "Nice to meet you, too. We've been waiting all day for you to get here."

Maggie and Janie moved awkwardly through the front door into the wide foyer. To the right was the living room, framed in dark wood, with a deep window seat looking out onto the yard, books piled on the side tables. Real paintings hung on the wall, sad landscapes of unfamiliar terrain, the oil paints clumping expertly to evoke the evening sunlight. A grand piano stood in the corner, sheet music billowing from the top. To the left was the dining room. The table was set with china. There were fresh flowers everywhere. The sisters stood motionless. Janie could only think of the movies, as though each room were a stage set waiting to reveal a particular drama. She never knew real people lived like this.

Kitty took their hands, "Maggie and Janie, I'll show you your rooms—give you time to freshen up before we eat. I know you must be tired. I know you've been through so much this past week. We are going to take good care of you here. Don't worry." Kitty, too, seemed like a part of the perfect scenery. Her face was powdered gently and yet Janie could still see the deep worry lines falling from her eyes, the anxious set of her neck.

She led them up the staircase, past formal black and white pictures of William, standing between his parents, first as a baby, then a toddler, one more as a little boy, his graduation picture, medical diploma, as if to say, "Here look—this is our life, first baby, then boy, then man."

"Now Maggie and Janie, I put the two of you next to each other. Now of course, Maggie, you will be joining William in his room soon enough!" Kitty laughed unaware of how Maggie stiffened, mortified. Kitty kept up her cheerful banter, "Sarah's room is right down the hall and my room is next to hers. Now I want you to make yourselves at home—you let me know if you need anything at all. This house is full of bedrooms—nine of them can you believe it? If you don't like the one I picked out for you just let me know and you can pick a new one, ok? There are extra blankets in the closet here if you get cold. I left some new soaps for you in the bathroom. Let me know if you need an extra sweater or a robe, or anything." Kitty stood in the doorway and awaiting their response, a tight, hopeful smile on her face.

"Thank you," was all Maggie could offer, Janie remained quiet, staring hard at the floor.

Maggie waited until Kitty had gone back downstairs and quietly walked back into her sister's room. Janie was sitting on the bed looking out the window into the back yard. Maggie went and sat next to her. "It'll be ok, Janie. I know it's strange now, but it'll be ok. I promise. I have to admit I didn't expect his mother to be anything like that, so so..."

"So scared," Janie said softly.

"No—not scared... like she was trying to... I don't know impress or something, win us over...Why did you say scared? I was going to say—overexcited, kind of desperate—not what I pictured."

"She wants William to be happy. You can tell. That's nice. She's his mother after all. They must have been lonely here—missed him," Janie leaned back into the pillow, closing her eyes.

"Lonely? No I don't think so. She just seems a little nervous," Maggie stood up.

"I'll see you downstairs."

Janie ran her fingers over the dark wooden bed frame, uncertain of whether or not she should unpack her clothes and place them in the dresser drawers. She got up and pulled her Daddy's sweater from her bag, burying her face in its stiff wool, longing for the familiar smell of home. She stood in front of the small mirror above the dresser and for the first time in months looked closely at her own face. She looked older, her face thinner. She wanted to crawl into the strange bed and finally cry, finally grieve all that she had left behind. It seemed like moments ago that she and Maggie were little girls, huddled under their big quilt, clutching their baby dolls, their bodies fitting together perfectly. But there would be no time for tears. Janie washed her face and walked down to dinner.

They were sitting together in the big living room. Maggie was relieved to see that Sarah was also sitting while William served them all a drink rather than serving them herself. Maggie watched her laugh and talk, reach out and take William by the hand. Why hadn't William told her about Sarah she wondered, this woman he clearly loved so much, who loved him, who lived here too? She wondered uneasily for the first time what else had not been revealed. In the company of those with whom he was most familiar, he suddenly seemed a stranger. Maggie sat anxiously on the edge of her cushioned seat. Janie stood awkwardly by her side until Kitty reached up and led her to the seat next to her.

"Come sit with me, Janie. Now listen, let me say first that I am so sorry about the death of your father. I'm sure you know that William lost his father too, my husband," Kitty paused, grasping Janie's hand, "I'm sure your father was a wonderful man. I'm sure you miss him. I thank him for the gift of his two daughters—the lord giveth and he taketh away—I am so thrilled that you have come here to live with us and I want you to feel like this is your home now. You can call me Kitty—everyone around here calls me by that name. Sarah and I have been living in this big house alone for too long and we are so happy to have it filled up again. Please make this place your home. Please feel comfortable."

She paused. Maggie and Janie were silent. "Well now—I think

we have a wedding to plan…" Kitty offered with an abundance of enthusiasm.

William cut her off. "No wedding to plan. We're going to City Hall on Monday, with you and Janie and Sarah as our witnesses. We want to be married. That's all."

"Monday?" Kitty answered startled.

Maggie could feel her cheeks go crimson. She waited for the argument, for the knowing glance at her stomach, for the scorn. But it didn't come. Kitty's eyes glistened with tears. She went to reach for Maggie's hand. Maggie smiled tightly, but did not reach out with her own.

Kitty flinched slightly, then recovered, "Well then, we might as well start the celebration now! Come on then, come sit at the table and eat. I know you must be starving."

Janie and Maggie followed Sarah and Kitty into the kitchen, insisting on helping them carry out the dishes. Maggie felt that already, instantaneously, lines had been drawn, Kitty referring her warmth and laughter to Janie, politely smiling towards Maggie. *It would be that way here, too,* she thought. Even here among strangers, a new place, a new beginning, Janie would be the one they would love.

Maggie was relieved to see Sarah join them at the table, too. Kitty, Sarah, and William carried the conversation, Maggie occasionally commenting quietly, answering questions when asked. Janie said nothing, unsure of how to eat, where to look. The food stuck in her throat. She kept fighting back tears, furious at her own foolishness. Kitty reached over to pat her shoulder countless times during the meal, perpetually keeping up pleasant conversation, unwilling to let anything go wrong this first night.

When dinner was finally over, William asked Maggie to take a walk with him in the gardens behind the house.

"Oh perfect, you too lovebirds go and we'll finish up. Such a beautiful night!" Kitty sang out.

Janie followed Kitty and Sarah into the kitchen. She moved

around in circles, trying to stay out of the way. She felt helpless, uncertain of how to perform even the most basic tasks in a house like this. She froze at the sink with a pile of dishes not knowing how she should wash them. Kitty came and took the stack from her. "Janie we've got this taken care of tonight. Make yourself comfortable. Go ahead—wander around. Make yourself at home. We'll finish up in here."

"Ok. Thank you," Janie reluctantly left.

She walked from room to room, stopping to look at pictures on the wall, the multitude of art and decorations, serving no purpose except to look pretty. She wandered until she came to the library, tucked in the far corner of the house. Janie ran her finger over the books' thick spines. She stopped and let out a gasp when she came across a title she recognized, *The Little Princess*, her memories of its pages stunning her, ghostlike. Sister Rosemary had read them this book. Janie remembered her hand resting on top of her stomach, feeling her daughter push against her as she listened to the story. She remembered how the little girl lost her father, how fate brought him back to her. She opened it and began to look through the illustrations, the characters coming back to her in vivid detail.

"Do you like that one?" Kitty's voice asked from behind.

Janie turned around startled, almost dropping the book.

"I'm so sorry if I scared you! *The Little Princess*—did you read that?"

"Yes... I mean no—I'm not much of a reader, but someone..." Janie stopped, feeling suddenly ashamed as tears once again burned in her eyes.

"Someone read it to you?" Kitty offered.

Janie looked up, so grateful to be rescued from any type of explanation. She shook her head yes.

"Your mother?"

"No, not my mother."

Kitty sat down. For the first time that night she looked relaxed, her face falling into comfortable, weary lines, her shoulders finally dropping.

"You know, Janie, my favorite thing in the world is to read stories aloud. My life has been one full of stories. I think I'd die from a lack of stories before I'd die from a lack of food. They nourish me—keep me going—always have. I'm an actress you know? Well, more of a director really—most of the time I help other people tell their stories. But anyway... William never let me read him this one even though I told him it was one of my favorites. He said it was for girls! I tried telling him it was my own father, a man among men, who read me this one—and he cried just as hard as I did at the end too... Would you mind if I read you a little bit? Indulge an old woman?"

Janie nodded yes.

"Have a seat there then. Best seat in the house."

Janie took a seat in the cushioned chair by the window.

Kitty sat across from her and began to read.

Maggie could see Janie's silhouette in the library window from outside. William held her hand, gently leading her around the yard, pointing out his climbing tree as a boy, the moon flowers that opened up at night, the tiny theater, darkened now, where his mother cast him in countless plays until he got old enough to say no. Maggie was silent. Finally, she couldn't hold back anymore.

"Why didn't you tell me about Sarah? You never told me anything about her."

William's face froze.

"It's just that—I didn't know how to explain, I wasn't sure if..."

"If what?"

"You see... Sarah started out as my mother's maid, but she isn't her maid anymore. They've been through a lot together. It's hard to explain. She is like another mother to me. She has always been like another mother to me. This is her home—as much as it's mine."

Maggie cut him off, "But you never said anything about her? Anything at all?"

William blushed, anxiously searching for an answer, "I—I didn't know if you would understand and so I thought I would wait—I would wait for you to meet her so you could see... I was worried that..."

"You were worried about how I would feel about a black woman living in your house who was like a mother to you? Wouldn't that have been important for you to know before you brought me here? Before you asked me to marry you? Before you asked me to come and live here? How I felt about something like that? Wouldn't that matter?"

William stumbled over his words, desperate to make things right, "I just thought I would wait... I knew that..."

Maggie cut him off, "You didn't know. You were worried about how your new wife from coal country would feel. Not a lot of black people up there, right? I can tell you now I feel fine. You didn't need to worry. I only feel sad that you didn't tell me, ever, about someone this important to you."

"I'm sorry. You're right…"

Maggie looked away, "I guess we don't know each other all that well after all."

William's face fell, stricken. He reached for her hand, "We know enough, Maggie. We do. I know we do," he answered pleadingly.

Maggie said nothing.

31

Janie awoke in her bed the next morning, taking in the strange room. The morning light filtered in, making patterns on the pale blue wallpaper. She had dreamed the most ordinary of dreams that night. She was making her daddy's bed, bottom sheet, top sheet, followed by the worn quilt. In the dream she had been so pleased by how clean the sheets were, how they had dried just so without any wrinkles. There had been no babies crying in this dream, no little girls asking desperately where she had gone, and yet still, on waking she had wept, silent tears, desperate for home. The permanence of her departure struck her cold. She dressed quietly, every action feeling unfamiliar, and made her way downstairs to the kitchen. Sarah was already there, making coffee.

"Good morning, " Janie said quietly from the door.

Sarah looked up surprised, "Good morning. You're up early. How did you sleep?"

"Fine."

Sarah began to pull flour and sugar from the pantry. Janie stood watching her.

"Can I help?" she asked softly.

Sarah stopped and looked at her skeptically, "Sure. Do you know how to cook?"

"Some things..." Janie answered suddenly unsure if what she had cooked for her Daddy every week even counted as food in a house like this.

"What do you like to cook?

"Soup?" answered Janie feeling foolish. "Some other things, too."

Sarah paused, taking in the small figure before her now. Janie's eyes waited nervously.

"Soup is good. Everybody should know how to make a good soup. It's a soup kind of day in fact—a little cold out there this morning. Come on—let's see what we have."

"Sarah?"

"Yes?"

"Do you live here all the time?"

Sarah put down the pot she had in her hands. She spoke firmly, "Yes. Yes I do. I consider this place my home, too." She stared straight into Janie's eyes, awaiting her reaction.

"I'm glad," Janie barely whispered.

Sarah was silent for a moment, "Well ok then. Let's have some breakfast and then we can talk about the soup."

By the time the others came down, Janie had familiarized herself with the kitchen. The window above the sink looked out onto the garden. To the right was a door that led into a washing room and the door to the back yard. The kitchen cabinets were bright yellow, matching the yellow kitchen booth, round, large enough to hold ten people. There were windows on either side of the room, one looking out at the bird feeders and one facing the circle of the long driveway.

Kitty walked in in coveralls with her hair up, totally transformed from the elegant woman who had greeted them at the door that night. She smiled when she saw Janie and Sarah together.

"Good morning. I'm sure Sarah is so glad to have your company here because I can't seem to cook anything right. I make up for it though in the garden, don't I Sarah? Come on, Janie, come with me a minute and have a look. We'll find a good spot for your Lilies of the Valley."

Janie washed the flour from her hands and followed Kitty out the back door. The backyard was enclosed by a high stone wall. In the far right corner was the theater, ivy crawling up its side. There were small stone paths connecting four different gardens, boxwood lining each one. There were roses, and hydrangeas, beds full of zinnias, morning glories stretching up twine. In four neat beds were the vegetables: tomatoes, kale, string beans, a wall of cucumbers, beets, eggplants. Janie followed Kitty as she pointed out each plant, listening quietly. She could see Kitty begin to relax, her practiced, upbeat banter, lightening as she lost herself in the description of her garden.

Finally she looked up. "I'm sorry. I've just gone on and on."

"It's ok—it's beautiful. I've never seen so many beautiful things in one place."

"Thank you... So—do you want to plant your Lilies of the Valley before they wilt away? I think I know a good spot. They will spread out like a magic carpet before you know."

Maggie watched from the window upstairs as Janie and Kitty worked on their hands and knees in the garden.

She wishes he loved her. He probably wishes it himself, she thought. *They always do.*

32

On Monday morning they all drove down to City Hall. Kitty had made each of them a beautiful bouquet of flowers despite William's protest.

"A wedding is a glorious occasion no matter where it takes place. Now you indulge your old mother," Kitty said while pinning a billowing rose on his lapel.

The judge who married them barely looked up as they said their "I do's".

William took Maggie into his arms and kissed her passionately.

"Thank you," he whispered softly into her ear.

William had to go straight to the hospital after the ceremony, promising to make it home that night.

Sarah, Kitty, Janie, and Maggie shared a quiet cab ride home.

Later that day, Kitty came and knocked softly on Maggie's bedroom door, where she had secretly gone to rest, her body becoming more acutely aware of the life inside her with each passing day.

"Maggie, do you mind if I come in?"

Maggie went to sit up, but Kitty came and sat on the bed.

"Now don't you get up. You rest. You and that baby need to rest."

Maggie said nothing.

"Don't worry—when you get to be my age you either think

you've lived long enough to understand exactly how the world works or you realize that you don't know a damn thing. I'm happily of the latter. I've decided to let life keep on surprising me each day. Yes I know you are going to have a baby and I wouldn't dare to think less of you or my son because of this beautiful gift. This house needs a baby. Now rest," Kitty patted the space on the bed next to Maggie, not daring to reach out to her again. She stood up awkwardly after a few moments.

"I'll let you sleep."

"Kitty?"

"Yes?" Kitty looked back, hopeful, expectant.

"Thank you," Maggie said firmly.

Kitty's face fell a little as she smiled tightly and closed the door.

That night, now in their own room in his mother's house, William undressed Maggie slowly, as if seeing her for the first time. He took her hand.

"Maggie—I'm sorry I never told you about Sarah. I should have. I don't want to have any secrets from you."

He was quiet for a while. Maggie began to feel uneasy, suddenly aware of her nakedness. She knew there was more to come.

"There is something I've got to tell you, especially now that we are going to have a baby. Something else I should have told you before. I'm sorry I waited until now. It's about my father. The story I told you, it was a story. It wasn't his heart, it wasn't his heart that killed him, it was his head. He fought hard his whole life, but I think he lasted long enough for me to become a man. One day he gave up, he couldn't fight his demons anymore. Put a pistol in his mouth the day after I graduated from medical school. My mother found him. He did all he could, Maggie, he was a brilliant doctor, but he couldn't keep those voices at bay. He tried, he tried in every way he knew how, but he couldn't. Putting that pistol down his throat was the only way he could find peace, the only way to make those voices stop. I worry about being his son, my mother does, too. But when I met you I knew, when I met you that very first time when you came yelling about that boy, that boy who was dying in the hospital, I knew then you would always know what the right choice was. I knew you would keep me safe. I knew you were strong enough to fight off anything." He collapsed into her arms, waiting for comfort. Maggie remained stiff.

She had wondered why this brilliant son of an artist had chosen her instead of so many other more cultured, more beautiful women. Why her, Maggie Coyle? She'd wondered too how she could fall so completely in love with someone so different. But now she knew. He was like every other man she had ever known, searching for someone to save his life. It wasn't love she had recognized in his eyes, it was desperation. She felt a small part of herself go permanently cold.

33

Maggie wasn't used to so much conversation, to people constantly asking her how she was, how she slept, what she thought. It unnerved her deeply. Kitty hugged William each morning when he came downstairs like he was still a small child. They told each other they loved each other daily while Maggie tried to hide her disgust. She grew quiet, distant, as though in protest to their practiced warmth. In the beginning, Kitty had gone to hug her every morning too, but even she had finally given up, instead forcing a fiercely joyful "Good Morning!" on Maggie the moment she appeared each day.

Maggie blamed her pregnancy for her moods, for the hours spent alone in her room. Janie watched as William would reach out his hand to her, hopeful, the same look of entranced desperation that she had seen on Joseph's face. Sometimes she imagined what it would have been like if they had loved her instead, the devotion and gratitude she would have given in return for being loved like this, openly, completely, without shame.

Janie tried to make herself useful, helping with the meals, cleaning, working in the garden, shadowing Sarah whenever she could. She stayed at the house, behind its stone walls, only listening to the sounds from outside, trolley cars, school children walking home for lunch, young boys hawking the evening bulletin.

Every day Sarah asked her if she wanted to come with her on her daily trip to the farmers market. Janie always politely replied, "No thank you." She hoped that Sarah would not take offense. She would run to meet her at the front gate to take her packages whenever she returned, so as not to appear lazy.

One morning as Sarah got ready to leave, after Janie once again politely declined to go with her, Sarah stopped. She put down her purse and sat down at the kitchen table with Janie. They were alone. Maggie was upstairs in bed, Kitty in the theater looking through costumes for her next play, William gone off to the hospital.

Janie sat stiffly as though awaiting punishment. Sarah finally began to speak softly, "Janie you're going to come with me today. Out. We are going to leave here like ordinary people and go to the farmers' market. We are going to go shopping for dinner together. I need your help."

Janie looked down and said nothing.

"I know..." Janie looked up startled, Sarah's face, mottled with freckles leaned in towards her, "I know you are afraid. I don't know why. You don't have to tell me why, but I know you are scared of going out there. You haven't left this house once since you came."

"I'm not scared..." Janie said, surprised by the anger in her voice. She couldn't say anything more. There was no way to explain to Sarah how painful it was to be in a new place, how every new experience here somehow seemed like a betrayal, a conscious act of leaving her daughter behind, a willing amnesia.

"I'm sorry." Words swelled inside of her. *I have left my baby behind. I don't want to see any more of the world than I have to without her.*

"Janie—I don't need to know to understand. Don't tell me sorry. And don't feel ashamed. You have nothing to apologize for. Lord knows I want to stay behind these pretty walls all day sometimes, too. I know what it's like to be afraid. But I've seen what happens to people who hide here, thinking they are somehow safe. The world has a way of getting at you no matter what. You have to keep yourself strong. That's why we've got to go out there. We are going to start by going to the market. Get your coat."

Janie nodded.

They stood at the trolley stop alone, Janie silent. The car approached and Sarah ushered Janie on, directing her to the first open seat. Janie looked out the window, marveling at the number of people, the grand houses set back from the road, the traffic.

It was a short trip to the farmer's market. It was housed in a low building across from the public high school. There were two butchers, three farm stands full of vegetables, the Amish farmers' wives selling pies, sticky buns. Sarah moved from stall to stall, recognized by all the vendors, filling her bags with the night's meal. Janie followed behind. There was a stall selling lace fabric, ornate chairs, rugs, and in the far corner an antique baby carriage with white linens lining the inside.

"Oh look!" said Sarah.

She pulled Janie over to the carriage. Janie couldn't resist running her fingers over the handles, imagining what it would be like to push it along, mindful of the baby inside.

"That would be so nice for your sister."

"Yes," Janie replied quietly.

"Maybe we'll come back for it—I'll tell Kitty."

Janie could only nod.

They stopped last at the butcher. Janie marveled at the abundance of meats, whole turkeys, sausages of every kind. She remembered her Mama cooking the left behind parts, the only ones she could afford, the smell of fat frying in the kitchen.

"Miss Sarah, what can I get for you today? And who is this lovely lady?"

"This is Janie Coyle. She is William's wife's sister and she's living with us now, too. From upstate."

"What town?"

"Mahanoy?"

"I have a cousin up near there. Coal country."

"Yes sir. My Daddy was a miner... He died this summer," Janie offered softly, unexpectedly.

"I'm sorry for your loss."

"Thank you," Janie answered awkwardly.

"Well—I know Miss Sarah and Miss Kitty will take good care of you. They might even try and put you in one of their plays too if you don't watch out! Now what can I get you ladies?"

Sarah carefully picked out the meat. When it was wrapped and she had paid she reached into her bag and handed the butcher a neatly wrapped package.

"These are from Kitty. More books," she smiled.

Janie could see the butcher's eyes change, darken with sadness, perhaps grief.

"Thank you—tell Kitty thank you, too. "

"He's in my prayers—always."

The butcher could only nod.

"Nice to meet you," Janie whispered.

Sarah led Janie outside to the trolley stop. While they waited she began to talk quietly.

"That man's only son is in prison. Murder. They are not going to kill him, but he is going to be in there for life. I think that might be worse than watching your son die, knowing he is rotting away in a place like that, because of his own sins. That butcher is a good man, too—he was a good father. I remember the little boy coming to work with him. Beautiful child. There is no justice in the world sometimes. Kitty sends him books," Sarah paused. "That woman thinks a good story can cure about anything."

The trolley approached noisily. Sarah and Janie climbed up the steps and squeezed into a vacant seat together. The warmth and strength of Sarah next to her made Janie feel sleepy, almost happy. She leaned her head against the glass.

When they got home, Kitty came and greeted them on the path leading up to the house.

"Janie I didn't know you went with Sarah. Did you like the market? Isn't it wonderful? Is there anything from home you haven't been able to find?"

"Yes," answered Janie, feeling the question's unexpected sting, panic rising up inside of her. She had been unable to shake her belief that somehow by leaving her town she had left her daughter's memory behind as well, as though this too could shrivel up, die.

Kitty watched her face fall, "What? Is there something you are looking for Janie?

"No. Nothing," Janie answered.

"Well you let me know if there is something you need? Okay? Anything."

Janie nodded.

They walked into the kitchen and started to unpack the groceries. Sarah waited until Kitty had gone back outside before she spoke.

"The world is going to keep on coming. We can't stop it. Tomorrow we'll go back out there again."

34

Sarah had been with Kitty since she was sixteen years old. Her own mother, Daisy, had worked for Kitty's mother her whole adult life. Daisy had her sights set high for her only daughter. She wanted Sarah to go to college. Sarah's father had died when she was four, fatally injured in a construction accident. Sarah was brought up in the tight community of domestics, all working in big houses, all lived in by white people. Sarah was never allowed to go out with friends on the weekend, couldn't even dream of going on a date. Her time outside of school was devoted to church and schoolwork.

Two weeks after her sixteenth birthday, a friend of her mother's who was going to visit relatives down south for the weekend asked Daisy if Sarah could come and help babysit for the family she worked for. She would be paid well. There was only one little boy, a sweetheart, and he would be napping most of the time. Daisy reluctantly agreed to let Sarah go. She rode the bus with her daughter to the house. "Remember, this is just a day job. You are never going to be anyone's maid. You can study while the little boy sleeps." Daisy lingered and watched Sarah walk up the drive, trying to ignore the fear that inexplicably crept up in her stomach.

They were young, a husband and wife. They were going to play tennis and then to have lunch, shouldn't be gone more than four, five hours. It was hot that day. Sarah could feel sweat sliding down her neck as she listened to the instructions. She was to give the little boy his lunch and put him down for a nap. He would sleep two hours, the mother said with authority.

He was beautiful, curly blond hair, blue, blue eyes. Sarah watched him eat his lunch of boiled peas and potatoes, carefully wiping his chin after each bite, so that nothing would mar his white shirt embroidered with red and blue sailboats. She carried him up to his room, gently removed his tiny shoes and socks, and read him a stack of books until he closed his eyes and took a deep breath, marking sleep. She left the door open so that she would hear him if he called for her.

She came back downstairs and cleaned up the rest of lunch. She looked at the clock. One hour and forty-five minutes before he was supposed to awake from his nap. She went and got her book from school. Shakespeare.

She never heard his little feet on the padded stairs, never heard the back door push open.

She went and checked on him after only an hour, his bed empty. Her search became quickly frantic, racing back and forth between the unfamiliar rooms.

It was only a tiny fish pond. In its center was a statue of a little boy with angel wings.

She spotted his white shirt from the upstairs window and first let out a breath of relief until she realized he wasn't moving. She sprinted down the stairs, still thinking she could save him. She gathered his wet body against her chest and ran to the closest house. She knew her mother's friend Anna worked next door. She brought him to the back door screaming.

Anna knew before Sarah did that the boy was dead. She wiped any trace of recognition from her face and silently went to get the owners of the house. The ambulance and the police were summoned, Sarah was left holding the boy on the back steps. No one from the house came near her or offered to take him from her arms.

Daisy arrived right after the police. The boy had finally been lifted from Sarah's arms, the shadow of his wet body stained across her dress. Sarah looked at her mother's face, transformed; she had never seen her so afraid.

"Tell me what happened before they come talk to you," her mother hissed gesturing towards the police.

"He was asleep. I was downstairs studying like you told me to. I went and checked on him after an hour and he was gone. I found him like this in the pond out back. Two hours his Mama said. She said he would sleep for two hours. I'm so sorry, mama, I'm so sorry…" she began to weep.

"Do not cry," was all that Daisy replied. "Do not make a sound."

When the police approached, Daisy stood in front of her daughter, answering their questions. Sarah could not control her shaking now.

"May we go?" Daisy finally asked.

"Yes. But where can I find you if I need to get in touch with you?"

"We will be at the Lane's house. I am their maid." Sarah looked up alarmed.

"Thank you."

They did not go home. Daisy walked her daughter straight to Kitty's mother's house. Sarah leaned in the door jam and watched her mother cry, beg for protection, forgiveness.

"Please let us stay here tonight. I am so sorry to involve you in all of this. It was just an accident. Please let us stay here."

Kitty's mother had paused long enough to leave them afraid, and then quietly agreed. There was a maid's room out back, until now unused. Sarah slept in the same bed as her mother that night, clinging to her as if she were still a small child.

The next morning Kitty's mother called Daisy and Sarah into her study. Her daughter had recently married. She needed a maid as well. Perhaps Sarah could go stay there for a while. Her daughter was alone. There were no children to care for she said pointedly.

Kitty was the baby of the family, the youngest by many years, coddled and protected. She had two older brothers busy with their own lives, families. Her mother had had her late in life, "a bit of an embarrassment" she used to say. Her mother was from an old Philadelphia family that she despised deeply and loudly to whoever would listen. Kitty's father, a wealthy banker, died suddenly from a heart attack three months before she was to be married. Her older brother walked her down the aisle as she wept, still stunned that her father was gone. He delivered her into the hands of John, her new husband, so eager to take over for her father, to take care of his new young wife.

Kitty's father had indulged her every wish. She had been a shy child, alone often, fascinated by stories and plays. He always encouraged her imagination, repeating countless times that a good imagination was the greatest gift one could have. He'd read stories to her throughout her life, changing his deep-barreled voice to match each character. Kitty shied from the stage but worked behind the scenes on every school play she could. Her father's wedding gift had been to have a theater built in the backyard of her stately new home, a gift her mother found both dangerous and stupid. She had hoped that married life would cure her daughter of her dreamy ways, her oddness. Her father never got to see the finished product. The theater was beautiful, all natural wood with a cedar shake roof, with seating inside for fifty.

Kitty's mother woke at noon, dressed for lunch, and then in later years, took her booze to bed with her early. Kitty had been mostly raised by Daisy. She knew Daisy had another daughter throughout her life, imagined this somehow secret sister of her own. She was startled when Sarah showed up unexpectedly at her door with Daisy and her mother. She hadn't asked for a maid, and yet she was happy for the company. Her husband was often away and even when he was home he often locked himself in his study.

Daisy and Sarah stayed on at Kitty's mother's house. Daisy could not shake the feeling that the police still might come for her daughter, still might find a way to blame her for the death of that tiny boy. When Sarah would return home from her day at Kitty's, the two of them would sit quietly together in the maid's room, both consumed with loss. The image of the lifeless boy followed Sarah relentlessly, the cold of his skin like scars on her fingertips. Daisy mourned as well, the death of the life she had hoped for for her daughter. They did not seek out their old friends, terminated the lease on the apartment Daisy had rented for twenty-three years, gathered their few belongings and hid from the shame, moving permanently to the Lane house.

Kitty had fallen madly in love with the first man who had been kind to her besides her father. He was a surgeon, a gifted one they said. No one knew that the quiet, mild mannered man, who so openly declared his love for Kitty was so sick. At the time, psychiatry was still considered akin to voodoo. His madness was his fault, his weakness, and so he hid it as best he could. Kitty, a novice when it came to marriage, to sex, to life, was left bewildered. Was it normal for a man to not come home for two days? Was it normal for her sweet husband to be prone to fits of violent rage? She wouldn't dare ask her mother. She kept to the guest room at night, rereading her favorite plays, *Macbeth*, *Romeo and Juliet*, finding comfort in the familiar printed words when the drama of her own life was intractable.

There was only Sarah, the only witness to this secret turmoil in her life. She rarely talked to Kitty, completing her duties quickly and accurately, creating tasks for herself when Kitty failed to provide them, leaving promptly at five to return home to her own mother.

The years passed, months of normalcy interrupted by a week of strange behavior, paranoid outbursts, constant demands by John. Kitty became pregnant. She announced the news to Sarah and watched as her face fell, as she stared hard at the ground.

"I will have to leave before the baby is born."

"Why? Why would you leave?" Kitty had asked.

Kitty waited out the silence. "The boy. The boy who drowned," was all Sarah could finally offer.

"That was not your fault. That was an accident. It could have happened to anyone… anyone at all. I need you here—please stay. Please stay here with me."

No one had ever uttered those words before to Sarah, not even Daisy—*not your fault*. Sarah realized how much she had longed to hear someone speak such forgiveness. She decided this was her chance, her opportunity to care for someone else, to protect them from harm, to erase the shame that still marred her every waking moment.

Kitty was to have only this one baby, a beautiful, brilliant boy, William. Sarah was by her side when he was delivered, at home. She was the first to hold him while the doctor tended to Kitty. She stayed over that night, and the next, ever vigilant. She never left.

For a time, after his son was born, John seemed okay. Kitty began to believe that her little boy was the answer to her prayers, what her husband needed to stay on track, to stay hopeful in this world. But her baby boy's magic spell lasted only two years. John disappeared the day of William's second birthday, fled amidst the beautifully wrapped piles of presents and the elaborate cake that Sarah had created. He didn't come back for three days. Sarah finally called on the gardener to search for him. When he had brought him home, tattered and dazed, the young man had been too shamed to tell where he found him.

Sarah and Kitty did everything in their power to protect William from his father's secret demons, his rage, but as William got older it became too difficult to hide. Kitty decided to send him away to school rather than have him be victim to his father's madness. She would sob the whole way home after dropping him off every year, cry into Sarah's shoulders at having been forced to abandon her boy. She believed she had no choice.

John got worse with every passing year. He would be carried home reeking of alcohol and another woman, crying out about those who followed him everywhere. Slowly, his madness began to creep out into the open. They stopped receiving invitations to dinner. He was quietly asked to step down from his position at the hospital. The women whom Kitty had considered her acquaintances stopped calling. Kitty was relieved.

And then there would be moments when John would return to her, so kind, so brilliant, a glimpse of the man she loved. She kept it a secret from William, telling him his father left the hospital to do research on his own, she kept it a secret until he grew up, until his Daddy died and then she could keep it no more. She was too afraid for her own beautiful boy. Finally she told him the truth.

"You must always guard yourself against such demons. You need to find someone who is strong enough to help you fight them off," she told him that night. *Someone stronger than your mother,* she thought silently.

It took her husband's death for her to begin a new life. He shot himself backstage in her theater. She would forgive him for much, but never for that.

It took finding his mangled face, blown to pieces in her quiet, sacred space, for Kitty to finally open up the theater doors to the outside world, to use the gift her father had given her in the way he had intended. The day after her husband's funeral, she and Sarah scrubbed every inch of the theater and began to search for and welcome anyone who wanted to play a part in their stories. Kitty was determined that her husband's death would not be the final act performed.

35

Sarah was to remain always single, childless. Kitty often felt like she had taken Sarah's life from her, demanding so much at such a young age. She believed that Sarah had saved her life, pulling her out of the darkest days, mothering her child when she could not.

Sarah's mother was to die apologizing to her, for not being able to protect her, for not being able to send her off into the world the way she had hoped. She couldn't have known how quickly Sarah's presence would become essential to Kitty's very survival.

The torment of Kitty and John's secret world was familiar to Sarah. She understood that every moment, no matter how tranquil, held the presence of danger. The well-mannered normalcy of those surrounding her, wishing her good morning, handing her change at the grocery store, walking idly on the opposite side of the street, could transform itself instantly into something vile, menacing. She too lived in a world of unpredictable, hidden demons.

When she heard the shot that day she knew, knew before she saw Kitty running, knew before they found John's body limp backstage, that he had left them, left the unrelenting torture of his world. Later she helped Kitty clean the remnants of his blood, the remnants of his life.

When Kitty decided to open the theater doors, Sarah joined her, helping to read the plays, to find actors, to make costumes, to create alternate, pliable worlds, the stories acted on stage somehow more true than the fiction of their reality. Sarah found an elusive type of freedom in these stories.

Sarah's mother used to tell her that in life there were those who had already seen the other side, wise souls among us whose suffering in this world allowed them a glimpse of the next.

"The eyes are the window to the soul," she quoted. As a child, Sarah used to gaze into the eyes of unsuspecting adults trying to see salvation until her mother told her that staring was rude and could be dangerous, too.

When Janie walked into their house for the first time, a small white girl, broken in so many ways, she looked shyly at Sarah, briefly letting her eyes linger. Sarah knew Janie had been there, too.

36

The baby came in late March. Janie and Kitty were out back planting lettuce in the cold frame, the promise of spring peeking out from the damp earth.

"Ah spring, Janie! Makes me happy to be alive, just having survived another winter. It's coming—tulips, the hostas, strawberries by the back door, warm sunshine in the morning, sweet peas, mint!" Kitty went on, a familiar soliloquy.

They looked up when they heard the kitchen door slam.

"Janie!" Maggie was holding fast to the side of the house, her skirt marked by wetness between her legs, her face frozen in terror. Janie knew then, took her hand, led her inside and slowly upstairs. She called down to Kitty to phone for a cab. She gently helped Maggie out of her wet clothes, her sister's bare stomach protruding with life, her nakedness now so unfamiliar.

Maggie stopped to grab her hand. The two of them stood alone in the room, holding each other silently. Janie looked at her sister's pale face, stricken with terror, and thought, *There you are, Maggie. After all this time, there you are again.*

Maggie spit out her words in a fierce whisper, "I don't think this is right. I don't feel right. I can't remember when I felt the baby move last. I don't think this is how it is supposed to be."

A brief moment passed where Maggie could have asked, *Was it like this when you had your baby? Were you afraid?* She could have said sorry.

"You're going to be fine. You're ok," Janie reassured her firmly.

When they went downstairs the cab was waiting, Sarah and Kitty holding on to each other in excitement, fear, standing by the open door. The contractions had already begun, Maggie gripping Janie's hand harder with each wave of tightness.

William greeted them at the hospital gates and they were surrounded instantly by nurses and doctors, all eager to help their new surgeon's young wife.

Maggie panicked as they surrounded her. "William, I want Janie to stay. I want Janie to stay with me—she needs to be there. William. Tell them please, tell them I want my sister to stay."

"Janie can stay. It's ok—she can stay with you the whole time," William looked with disbelief at his wife, so suddenly young, shaken. He felt fear swell inside of him. He watched her pass through the double doors, fighting the urge to pray.

There were so many nurses and doctors, all wishing her well, assuring her she was going to be fine, telling her how highly they thought of her husband. So many voices. Janie never let go of her hand. She knew what Maggie was thinking, knew whose face she was seeing, knew the voices and the silence she remembered. Janie knew what she needed to say.

"This baby is fine. This baby is just fine," She repeated the words endlessly, throughout the many hours of contractions, the long night, the final pushes at dawn that brought Maggie's baby into this world, alive.

Her body was warm and wet, still covered in Maggie's blood. The soft whimpers falling from her mouth were testimony to her breath, her voice, her life. Her baby was a girl. This was not what Maggie had wanted. Girls were weak, catty, stupid, left behind, tired, used, desperate, easily damaged, discarded. Girls were like her Janie. Maggie had prayed for a boy even though she knew she shouldn't.

"Pray that it's healthy," the nurses used to say. Maggie would nod her head yes, but think no. She wanted a boy.

But this baby girl, already sucking forcefully at her breast, clutching her mama's loose strand of hair, still covered in her mama's blood, this baby girl was strength itself. Maggie reached for Janie and pulled her close, her baby girl, held softly between their two chests.

"Thank you," was all Maggie could say, though her heart surged with longing for forgiveness.

"She is beautiful," Janie whispered.

Janie reached down to make sure the baby was swaddled close to Maggie's chest, secure next to her mother. No one would take her away.

Maggie felt the soft weight of her daughter, marveled at her life, her open eyes, already searching.

37

They named the baby Veronica, after Maggie's mother. It was William's idea, expressed in front of Janie. Maggie could find no way to explain without cruelty how desperately she would rather choose another for her firstborn, an unfamiliar name, devoid of any history. They called her daughter, Bonnie, like everyone had called her mother, too. It seemed a miracle to say this name aloud again, to repeat it without sorrow to others.

The baby's umbilical cord fell off when she was twelve days old. Maggie was changing her diaper when it happened, revealing the perfect round mark of her belly button.

"Her cord came off!" Maggie gasped, holding the shriveled piece of root-like skin.

Kitty rushed over to see. "Oh good! We'll bury it out back in the garden! Our gift to Mother earth. It's good luck to do that you know? I read that somewhere... I'll plant something special with it... I know! A magnolia tree—there is nothing more beautiful than a magnolia tree. Those white flowers—heaven sent!"

"We can give her a bath now," Janie said quietly, remembering this fact from her baby book. She wondered what happened when her daughter's cord fell off, her last connection to her mother. Had they buried it? Tossed it in the trash? Had anyone even seen it fall?

Did she like her first bath? Janie let her fingers pass gently over Bonnie's bare stomach.

"We can?" Maggie looked at her incredulously, suddenly anxious.

Sarah answered for her, "Yes—of course we can! Let's do it now! I'll get the sink ready! I still remember William's first bath in this sink—we were so scared!"

"I was scared. I thought you knew just what you were doing!" laughed Kitty.

"Not a clue."

"I'll go and get her things, a towel, some soap, lotion? Anything else?" Kitty hurried off.

"Really? Now? But I just changed her diaper," Maggie said.

"We'll just change it again—she'll love it," Sarah said.

Sarah washed down the deep white porcelain kitchen sink. Kitty brought a thick towel, white baby soap, powder, a fresh nightgown.

"Now Janie you stand here ready with the towel for when she's done."

Maggie removed Bonnie's diaper, her legs kicking, her arms reaching upwards.

"Now come on, bring her here, the water is just right," Sarah called.

Maggie held her and began to place her in the water. Kitty put her hand in to help support her head. Sarah began to pour water on her belly from a small, tin cup. Janie stood and watched the six hands, immersed in the water, holding up the baby. Bonnie looked up at the three faces staring over her.

"Oh my."

"She is so beautiful."

"Look at her little legs go in the water."

"Twelve days old and look how alert she is, those eyes are taking in everything."

Sarah put a tiny bit of soap on a washcloth and handed it to Maggie.

"I got her. Go ahead. Wash her little belly. Under her neck, too."

"Not even fussing a bit."

Sarah poured the water over her again, washing away the soap.

"Now lift her out."

"I'm not sure I can," said Maggie.

"We'll help. Lift her out and hand her to Janie to wrap up. Then we'll lay her right on the kitchen table."

Maggie lifted the baby out of the water, her hands supported by Kitty's and Sarah's.

Janie stood waiting with the towel. She wrapped Bonnie up, the small weight of her body against Janie's shoulder unleashing a desire so deep, Janie felt as though she would cry out.

"Nothing more beautiful than a freshly washed baby," Kitty said, eyes transfixed on her granddaughter.

Sarah took the swaddled baby from Janie and placed her on the kitchen table as they gathered round. They watched as Maggie dried her off, making sure to reach the small folds in her legs, under her arms.

"Is she still wet?" Maggie exclaimed as the baby's fingers passed over her wrist.

"No, she's dry," said Sarah.

Maggie gasped, "It's her fingers—it's her fingers—they're so soft when they brush against my skin it feels like water, like raindrops— Janie put your wrist here—feel."

Janie put her hand out and felt the baby's fingers glide across her skin. It was like her sister said, like rain, warm summer rain, as though Bonnie didn't yet belong to the human world, as though she were a child of fairies, born of magic.

They all stood taking turns feeling the baby's touch glide over their skin.

Janie watched their faces, their wonder, their adoration. She had worried that her heart would grow cold once she saw her sister with a baby in her arms, that her longing would be unbearable. She had planned to leave soon after the baby was born, quickly returning to the Patch, away from her sister and her joy. Her longing remained undiminished, and yet she loved this baby, fiercely, desperately, inexplicably. She knew then she would stay.

Bonnie began to fuss. Sarah handed her to Maggie to feed again. Maggie could feel the rush of warmth to her breast, the way her head lightened in a way that reminded her of the subtle rush of whiskey. She watched as the baby drained each breast, feeling her energy slowly fade. Janie took her from Maggie's lap when she was finished.

"Go rest. Go on. I've got her now."

Kitty and Sarah chimed in, "Yes—go rest—go ahead up."

As Maggie walked up the stairs she could here them laughing. Later, staring straight at the high ceiling, she listened to Janie sing one of their mother's songs, stealing from her her daughter's first lullaby.

She awoke hours later, her breasts hard with milk. When the baby needed to be fed, simply nourished, her small fists desperately clawing the air, her anxious wail penetrating the thick walls, Janie brought her back to her mother.

38

Father Timothy had been sent away, away to Philadelphia, a city he had never seen before. His parish was on the outskirts of the center of the city, miles from the historic red brick buildings so fabled in this country's start.

The parish was teeming with children. Uniformed boys and girls flooded the school's classrooms, sixty, seventy, sometimes eighty to a room, spilling over each other, sharing desks, pencils, a sea of life. The school was set behind the church, a few blocks off the wide, grey boulevard, Roosevelt Boulevard, named after Theodore Roosevelt. At the intersection near the corner of the rectory stood a plaque inscribed with Roosevelt's famous words.

It is not the critic who counts; not the man who points out how the strong man stumbles, or where the doer of deeds could have done them better. The credit belongs to the man who is actually in the arena, whose face is marred by dust and sweat and blood; who strives valiantly; who errs, who comes short again and again, because there is no effort without error and shortcoming; but who does actually strive to do the deeds; who knows great enthusiasms, the great devotions; who spends himself in a worthy cause; who at the best knows in the end the triumph of high achievement, and who at the worst, if he fails, at least fails while daring greatly, so that his place shall never be with those cold and timid souls who neither know victory nor defeat.

Even more than scripture, these words, set against the grey slate, unnoticed by the countless downtrodden souls that walked past it daily, these words placed here, made him remember Jesus, gave him a kind of hope. He would linger there on his daily walk through the neighborhood, feeling the rush of cars pass him by.

The rectory was connected to the school by a small courtyard. When Father Timothy first arrived he tried to hang up his feeders there, but the street cats were too prevalent. He tired of finding the small birds' bodies left at his door, like gifts. He took the feeders down.

The other priest, Father Peter, was beloved by the children. He was a tall man, dark hair, a beautifully chiseled face, utterly confident in his swagger, conversation, faith. His handsomeness seemed to make his choice to follow Jesus all the more sacrificial.

The children would swarm around Father Peter when he walked into the courtyard before school in the morning. He knew all of their names, lifting them up into the air, laughing, throwing the football expertly with the groups of boys, cheeks flushed, eyes joyous. Father Timothy fell silent in his presence. He envied the ease with which Father Peter inhabited every room, every space, every sanctuary, always finding himself among friends.

There were always children in the rectory, children helping to sweep up, to prepare for mass, to water the plants out front, children longing for a morsel of attention from Father Peter himself, for a moment to bask in his warmth. They averted their eyes when Father Timothy approached. Father Timothy followed Father Peter's every directive, hoping to avoid mistakes, scrutiny.

Every Sunday after the regular mass Father Timothy would walk with Father Peter to the nut house, as the children called it, crossing the pulsing boulevard, hoping to bring God to the anxious, the unwell, the crazed.

Father Timothy would feel his heart race as the gates lifted, revealing the silent, looming institution, ushering in the two holy men.

Even here among the stench of urine, of men confined, of the subtle smell of burnt flesh, a reminder of failed attempts to eradicate, tame their madness, even here Father Peter glowed. He would open his bible and walk from man to man, reading prayers, repeating words of comfort. Like children, the men awoke in his presence. Father Timothy, silent, would follow him, bible in hand.

On their third visit Father Peter had spoken up.

"You need to go out among these men yourself this time. There is no need to be afraid. They are all children of God."

Father Timothy could only nod in agreement, fear rising in his throat.

That Sunday, in the corner was an old man, sitting with his back to the windows, eyes vacant, body soft, frail with confinement. He appeared safe.

Father Timothy approached, "Would you like to hear some prayers?"

The man did not look up.

"Sir, would you like me to read you some prayers today?"

He lifted his head slowly, eyes finding Timothy's, face transforming, as though in recognition, mouth curling to form forgotten words.

"Fuck your mother," he crooned.

Timothy turned to retreat, but it was too late.

"Fuck your mother," he repeated more loudly, white spit forming on his lips, unused to speech.

Father Timothy continued to walk away as the rant grew louder, his face crimson, the bible clutched fiercely in his hands, mortified at his shaking rage, the instantaneous pain this stranger, this lunatic had somehow unleashed. He could not prevent the thought that kept repeating itself in his head, though he knew it defied reason, *How dare he talk like that about my mother!*

Father Peter approached.

The man began to try to stand up, his hand waving towards Timothy, his robe falling open, his anger unabated by Timothy's retreat.

Father Peter went to the man, took his hands in his own, guided him firmly to his seat and held him there until he tired.

"You don't want to hear prayers today, old man? How about something else? How about if I sing something for you? Let's see."

Father Peter began to sing while still holding the man close, as though rocking a child.

"Into every life some rain must fall..."

He hadn't chosen to sing a church song. The old man's form softened.

Father Timothy felt the shame welling inside of him, unfit to stand in even the shadow of this man of God.

They walked home in silence.

They continued to visit every Sunday. Father Peter did not ask Timothy to walk among the patients anymore. Instead he sat and read assigned prayers softly from a book to a closely watched, heavily drugged group of patients, while the floor nurses looked on attentively. They did not want him to do any harm.

39

He had left the rectory as soon as he got the message, taking the bus to the hospital, Pennsylvania Hospital, the best in the city, they said. Father Peter's voice on the phone was tense as he told Father Timothy to hurry, that the injured man might not have much time, that his mother, a loyal parishioner, was there waiting. Father Peter had been called to a meeting with the visiting bishop, an honor he could not turn down. Father Timothy would have to make this visit alone. He could tell by Father Peter's voice that he was anxious, afraid that Father Timothy would fail yet again at bringing comfort to his people.

The woman's son had shot himself, and yet somehow survived. It was as though, at the last moment, he had a change of heart. "A change of heart," she had repeated incessantly on the phone to Father Peter. She believed her son meant to turn the gun away.

The bullet had taken part of his skull. The downstairs neighbor was the one who found him, who heard the shot followed by the dull thud of her son's body hitting the wooden floor.

William was getting ready to go home for the night, home to Maggie, to his new baby girl, Bonnie, when they called him down from the ER. A young man had tried to take his own life. He had used a pistol. Unbelievably, he was still alive. William, the hospital's new young surgeon, was already regarded as one of their best. They called him a miracle maker. When the injured man came in, when his heart was still beating, of course he was the one to call. Could he come and evaluate whether or not they should operate? Was there hope?

William pressed his shaking hands to his side as he took the elevator down. He had never seen a suicide before, amid all the horrors in his training, severed limbs, bodies mangled by machines, disease, he had never seen a body damaged by one's own hand. His father's body was already burning by the time William got the call, his blood washed clean from his mother's stage.

The young man's mother had been called from work. She lived alone two blocks from Father Timothy's church. This was her only son. He had moved out some years back, but he had trouble. He drank too much. The mother often baked cookies for Father Timothy and Father Peter. They were cinnamon with a layer of light, white frosting. Every time she delivered them she repeated that they were her son's favorite. This was all Father Timothy knew about the dying man. He liked cinnamon cookies.

William tried to clear his mind, to see only the body, the measures of the young man's pulse. Sweat gathered on his upper lip, glistened there, but William was unwilling to raise his hand to wipe it clean, afraid that the other doctors would notice his steady hands, a surgeon's hands, shaking. He would think later that he should have let him go, should have closed the wound only to save his mother the sight of her son's mangled head, but they were watching him and waiting and he had made the decision to operate. "He is young," he said, "...with a strong heart." And so they prepared the operating room.

William repaired what he could, but the damage proved to be too much. He knew before he completed his final stitches that the man would die. Her son's change of heart had come too late.

Father Timothy was waiting for William outside of the man's recovery room. The sight of the anonymous priest standing outside the room enraged William, the memory of his father's death by his own hand, returning with vicious clarity.

When William had received word that his father was dead he was stunned. Though he had seen his father's decline, watched as he fell further and further out of touch with his mother and the world around him, it had never occurred to William that he was so very sick. Despite Kitty's and Sarah's cheerful banter at every visit, he knew his father was not well, but he never feared he would lose him like this. He had seen sadness like his father's before, sadness that rendered the body immobile, like a deadly virus. He had felt the weight of it himself sometimes too, waking in the morning as though a granite slab lay on his chest, every fear he had appearing to come to fruition. And yet, he had no idea that his father would choose death, choose a pistol in his throat, to this other burden. William was terrified.

He had no friends, no brothers or sisters to call. His mother and Sarah had told him to wait until the next day to come home, sparing him the clean up, the shame. Out of desperation, he had walked to the nearest church, thinking that now of all times, would be the right time to pray. The priest was inside preparing for the next morning's mass.

"Can I help you?"

"I'm sorry. I'm not a member of this parish. I just found out that my father died and I want to say a prayer for him, please, if that's ok."

"Of course, come in. I'll pray with you."

William felt so grateful as he approached this man, someone who would know how to grieve, to comfort.

"Have a seat, son." They were silent together for a while in the quiet sanctity of the church. The priest spoke, "How did your father die?"

William looked up, relieved to unburden himself of such shocking news.

"He took his own life. With a gun. He shot himself in the head.

My mother said he has been unwell for a long time. I didn't know he was so sick," he nearly wept with guilt. How could he not have known? He would have to find a way to ask forgiveness, too.

"He took his own life?" the priest asked.

"Yes."

The priest was quiet again for a while before he spoke, "I am sorry, son. Your father's death was a sin. His life belonged to God. It was not his to end."

William watched as the priest's face transformed before his eyes. What he had seen as kindness now appeared to be mockery. He was reminded of the boys at school, their lilting refrain, "Your daddy is as crazy as a loon!"

William willed himself to speak up, "I am not surprised I guess. Your God let my father live in hell on this Earth. I wouldn't think that he would spare him in the afterlife. I don't know why I came here. My father was a good man. He was sick. If there is a God, he had left him, left his life, a long time ago. My father knew no comfort from your all powerful God." William stood up and walked out. He vowed never to set foot inside a church again.

Father Timothy remained waiting by the door to the recovery room. He spoke first, "Excuse me, Doctor, I am Father Timothy. I am a priest in his mother's parish. How is he?"

"He is going to die," William answered coldly.

Father Timothy said nothing for a while. His voice stayed soft, anxious, "And it is true, he took his own life?"

William answered loudly, "Yes. He killed himself with a gun. Why?"

The priest was silent, searching for the right words.

William could feel his rage growing as the image of his father wandering across the yard reappeared in his mind, his tattered robe blowing in the wind, like that of a dethroned king, his mother following at a safe distance, quietly pleading with him to come inside, come inside out of the cold.

"Daddy doesn't have any shoes on!" he shouted to Sarah, his face pressed against the cold glass of the kitchen window. He watched his father's bare feet sink into the freshly fallen snow.

Sarah answered hurriedly, "He's coming in—don't worry. Come on over here with me and help me make this orange juice."

Sarah had picked him up and led him over to the juicer, the counter filled with fresh oranges cut in half. She placed the orange on top of the juicer and turned on the machine, placing her hand on top of William's. The noise from the juicer was deafening, drowning out the sounds from outside, his mother's pleading voice, her struggle to bring his father out of the cold, her steady encouragement, edging him near the fire.

William watched the juice flow out, Sarah's hand keeping his steady, quickly moving through the pile of sweet oranges.

By the time they finished, the house was quiet again. His mother sat in the other room with his father, tending to his blistered, raw feet. William came and sat near her. Sarah brought his father a glass of juice.

"Thank you," his father had whispered.

Father Timothy still had not spoken, small beads of sweat appearing on his forehead. William's voice was menacing when he spoke again, "Why do you need to know if this man killed himself? Why? So you could deny him a Christian burial? Because he dared to do what God would not? To end his own suffering?"

"No... I—it does matter—it does matter to the church. But I..."

William cut him off, "Father can I ask you something?"

"Yes," Father Timothy replied anxiously.

"I would think that a benevolent God would have come to this man sooner in his suffering, would have spoken to him before now. Don't you agree? I should tell you that I don't believe in your God. I have met the Devil many times in my operating room, in the heart of a healthy seven year old boy that suddenly stops beating, in the mangled body of a mother of five children who was just on her way to buy milk when the car hit her. Have you ever seen a tumor up close, Father? Seen the way it slowly spreads, kills? I've seen the Devil many times, but neither God nor his long suffering son Jesus have ever shown their face. You can believe what you want about suicide and sin, but I am ordering you to tell this man's mother that he will find salvation. In this hospital, I'm God. Do you understand?"

"Yes," Father Timothy wanted to say more, longed to tell this man that he was not here to judge, that he could not even offer compassion, that unlike the doctor, he was no healer. He was as lost as the dead boy. He watched William walk away.

Father Timothy remained motionless, filled with dread, at the entrance to the man's room. He fought the urge to leave, to run out of the hospital, to the anonymity of the streets outside, zipping his coat to hide the mark of his collar. No one expected healing from a common man.

He forced himself to enter the room. The man's mother stood to greet him.

She began to speak immediately, "I don't think he meant to do this, Father. I think it was a mistake. If he had meant to he wouldn't have lived this long. He would have died on the floor. There was a girl. She lived there. She broke his heart. He was a heartbroken man. But he must have changed his mind. God must have spoken to him at the last moment, helped him to escape sin. It was an accident. Please, Father... he is my only child."

Father Timothy went to take her hand. As he did, Father Peter appeared in the doorway. The woman turned away from Father Timothy.

"Father Peter," she said, relieved. He wrapped her in his arms repeating softly, "He is with God, no more suffering, he is with God." The mother shook with her sobs.

Father Timothy left quietly.

40

It was a Tuesday night. Father Timothy visited families in his parish every Tuesday. They could not disguise their disappointment at seeing his face at the door as opposed to Father Peter's. That night, he was turned away at the last house, measles, they said, hurrying him off, wishing him well.

He returned to the rectory early. It was dark. He entered the side door through the small kitchen. Down the hall he saw light escaping beneath the library door. The glimmer of light drew him forward. He pushed open the door to the library quietly, unconsciously hoping to not yet be revealed.

He recognized the smell at once, a noxious odor, the memory of which awoke a tremor in his chest.

Father Timothy knew the boy. His name was David. He was seven, a purple birthmark covering his right cheek, his nose running perpetually.

Father Peter was helping the boy button his pants, wiping the warm tears that fell quietly down his small face with a fresh handkerchief.

"Hello."

Father Peter looked up.

"Father Timothy. Hello... Run on home now, David. Tell your mother I will stop by tomorrow to see her."

David left quickly, eyes on the floor, careful not to look at Father Timothy as he walked through the door.

Father Timothy watched him walk away. He stepped inside the library and closed the door. Father Peter stood to arrange some scattered books on the shelf.

"Father Peter."

"Yes?"

"I know."

"Know what?"

"I know what you were doing, doing to that little boy."

"What are you talking about?" Father Peter looked up, his joyous eyes dark, transformed, as though possessed.

"I know," Father Timothy repeated, trembling.

"What do you know? I would stop now before you say more because I am sure you do not know what you are talking about. You have no idea, " answered Father Peter his voice menacing, unfamiliar.

Father Timothy persisted, "I do know. I know what was happening. It's not right. You can't do that to a child. I know what you were doing."

"How do you know?"

"I know," Father Timothy answered, pleadingly, heartbroken. Father Peter was silent, his eyes set on Timothy, unwavering.

The holy man spoke at last, unafraid. "And who are you to judge?"

"Father Peter, he is a child."

"She was, too, I hear."

Father Timothy fell silent, nauseous with disgust.

Father Peter left the room. Timothy stood paralyzed, his soul absorbing the scent of another man's sins.

It took only three days for Father Timothy's transfer orders to arrive.

41

There were to be five more children. Six babies in ten years, first three girls and then three boys, Bonnie, Charlotte, Ann, William, Jeffrey, and Michael. Years of sleepless nights, of days filled with cooking food, soothing tears, washing clothes, falling into bed at night so tired, making love with William, half awake, dream like. Afterwards Maggie would feign sleep, avoiding his eyes and the grateful desperation that still lingered there, that he perpetually described as love. When William finally slept, she would quietly get up and go check on the children, leaning into their faces, breathing their warm, sweet breath, always finding at least one asleep in bed with Janie, cocooned in her embrace.

"Keep them safe," she would whisper over and over, a prayer to her mama.

They were beautiful, her babies. She never let herself think how lucky she was, never said it out loud, not even in private with William, certain that doing so would break whatever kind of accidental magic had mistakenly been cast on the life of Maggie Coyle, a coal miner's daughter. She knew her heart was never so pure as to deserve such a gift.

She imagined every possible disaster, as though this would somehow offer her babies some kind of protection. Tragedy struck stealthily, in unexpected moments, bringing unseen, unimagined horrors, and so Maggie vividly imagined all that could possibly go wrong, all that could bring them harm. She would be vigilant. She would do everything she could to keep grief away. She could not afford to laugh with them like Janie, or proclaim her love aloud for everyone to hear, believing that this would only dare the universe to take one from her. Fear would be her greatest weapon.

William was rarely home. He rose quickly through the hospital, becoming its youngest chief of surgery in its history. He took on the most desperate, complicated surgeries. When he saved a life they called him a genius, a hero. When he lost someone, the families still felt comforted that their loved ones had been in the hands of the best. It was a time when surgeons were gods, their sutures nothing less than the work of mystics. When William would come home for dinner, briefly, before returning again to the hospital to finish rounds, he would get a hero's welcome. The children hugging him, all yelling at once, dancing around to steal his attention, narrowly missing the piles of food, Janie and Maggie and Sarah, brought to the table, his eyes locked on Maggie as he wandered through their embraces. Kitty had fabricated a million tales around their father, stories to fill the quiet gaps of their loneliness, their longing.

Their house was always full of visitors passing through. Actors and actresses that Kitty invited to stay on in the back house while working on a play. "The Upstaters," distant kin from the coal region that Janie encouraged to come visit, often staying on for weeks, months at a time. William welcomed them all into his home, grateful for their presence, grateful for the noise always filling his mind, drowning out the other more menacing voices from within.

He remained perpetually restless. One Saturday he drove them all to the mountains, having bought a cabin he'd heard about from another doctor, set back deep in the woods, accessible only by a dirt road strewn with rivulets. On the weekends, when he could get away, he would take them there, spending hours walking the trails, searching for the pileated woodpecker, following its tapping sound, lost in thought. At night, still sleepless, he would wander the moonlit paths listening for the snowy owl. Maggie would watch him from the window, resentful of his dreaminess. The woods were full of even more dangers for her children, rattlesnakes and coyotes in the summertime and in winter, the menacing call of the deep echoes of the lake ice shifting as her privileged children skated in circles laughing, unversed in tragedy.

The woods reminded Janie of home. She taught the children how to bait a hook, how to stand back from the creek so the trout couldn't see their shadow, how to pull a clump of moss to cover the fish to keep it fresh for the walk home.

"Do you remember how Daddy would slice open their bellies? How they would make that popping sound? How we would cry if there were fish eggs, saying we killed the mother? Do you remember that?" Janie asked while gently stroking the speckled fish as though it were a kind of talisman.

"No, I don't remember," Maggie answered, watching her sister's face fall. By day the children would collect the golden salamanders that raced over the damp creek beds. They would name them, making homes for them out of old shoeboxes, orange crates, encouraging them to race across the cabin floor. When Bonnie was little she would try to tuck the small creatures into beds she had made out of matchboxes where they would inevitably die. While she was sleeping, William would drop their lifeless bodies back into the woods like a trail of breadcrumbs leading home. The next morning, Kitty would create elaborate stories about the woods fairies coming to release them so that Bonnie would stop her crying.

William bought a summer house on the beach in New Jersey, too. The front window looked clear out onto the ocean. Kitty would set up an easel under an umbrella and spend her days trying to paint the sea. Sarah would stay on the porch, taking in the sea of white bodies at the ocean's edge.

The children loved the house at the beach best. They would race to the water the moment their car pulled into the sandy driveway, spilling out the open doors, leaving their shoes behind. Maggie and Janie would follow them, clinging to each other in the surf, having never learned to swim. Maggie would desperately try to call the children closer to shore, to safety, but they never listened, swimming effortlessly over and under each wave.

As the sun dropped towards the bay, the light would suddenly change. Janie and Maggie would sit together on the sand, watching the suntanned children race the waves to shore. It was like watching a memory in motion, their beautiful silhouettes against the ocean, so alive and yet fleeting.

Later on, Maggie would wonder why she never spoke up, why she never once spread her hands out in front of her, taking in the ocean, and said, "Janie, just think, two girls from coal country sitting here now."

Part of her knew that every time those children raced laughing up to shore, every time she stopped to count heads, finding momentary relief that they all were safe, Janie was still left searching for the one who went missing.

42

The first time she held Bonnie, Janie felt her heart surge. In her tiny lips, her furrowed brow, she perpetually found traces of her infant daughter's face. Alongside the pain, the searing longing that pulsed inside of her when Bonnie was first in her arms, there was the intoxicating joy of recognition. She took every opportunity to pick her up, whispering sounds of comfort, singing songs to her that their Mama used to sing, words emerging from deep within her consciousness, a pocketful of hibernating memories. Maggie stayed silent.

Janie stood by Maggie with every birth, marveling at the joy of a new life, a new baby to love, finding in each new tiny face something reminiscent of her own daughter. *She has her nose. He has her thick hair.* Her arms stayed filled with her sister's babies. She never feared for Maggie's children, somehow believing her own sacrifice had been enough for both of them. They would be safe, the universe would not dare to take another.

"*Que sera, sera. Whatever will be will be, the future's not ours to see, que sera, sera...*"

Janie sang this song countless times to each child, a song their Daddy sang to them growing up. She could remember him waking them at night, drunk, smelling of cigarette smoke, spilled liquor, the winter air, the lingering dampness of the mines, ignoring the whispered pleas of their mother, gathering his girls in his arms to tell them how much he loved them, singing the song that made him feel most unburdened. *Que sera, sera, what will be, will be.* Like their mother, Maggie stayed silent, as though the song itself were in protest of her vigilance, her efforts meant only to keep them safe from harm.

"I never liked that song," Maggie said softly as she watched her first son fall asleep in Janie's arms to its rhythm. Janie continued to sing.

Janie knew her life appeared abundantly empty, lonely to everyone else. She sensed their pity, their careful selection of words at times. William and Maggie, prodded by Kitty and Sarah, awkwardly arranged dates with suitable young men.

"After all—you're still young," Maggie had said pointedly. There were long, torturous dinner parties given by colleagues of William, where Janie could see the look of crumpled disappointment appear on her prospective date's face the moment he met her, the beautiful Maggie's sister. She could imagine the talk later, over scotch, whispered away from William, "Looks nothing like her older sister— name suits her—plain Jane if I ever saw one!" and the laughter that would follow. Worse though, were the nights where her prospective suitors had too much to drink, leaning into her with warm breath, unable to disguise their desperation, their need for anyone. Janie would go still with fear, quiet rage, waiting to be rescued by William who would take her firmly by the arm and lead her to Maggie. After a while, they all stopped trying.

Every Thursday Janie took the bus back upstate, two hours up and two hours back. As the children got older they begged to go with her, to this secret town, home to so many of her stories, but Janie found a way to say no. Thursdays were her day of solitude, pilgrimage. The bus let her off in the center of town.

She would walk first to the hospital. Alice would meet her in the cafeteria, a cup of coffee with a saucer on top to keep it hot and a powdered doughnut already waiting. Janie would bring photos sometimes, drawings by the children, stories of their lives. There would always come a moment of silence before they began, each one getting a chance to remember her own child, a chance to say aloud how old they would be now.

"He would be thirteen. I bet he would be tall like his father."

"She is nine and a half. God willing."

Together they would imagine their lives, what might have been.

"I sometimes think what I miss the most is his smell. I can conjure it up so clearly in my mind, but it's gone from this world. I've caught myself burying my face in a bushel of corn once at the market, something about the just picked husks made me remember him—but it was only a small part, a hint of my baby, just enough to make me stand foolishly in that store with my face pressed into a basket of corn."

Janie eyes filled up. "I've dreamt many times that I was walking down the street when a little girl passes me. I smell her first. Like an animal. I know it's her before I recognize her face. I wake up gasping for air."

When Alice's break ended they would stand and hug goodbye, lingering in each others arms, exchanging God love yous, Janie pressing money into Alice's hands despite her protests, always bringing a coat or a purse, or a piece of jewelry she claimed she thought looked better on Alice, or didn't fit her right.

They parted ways in the lobby. Alice headed down the basement to the cleaning supply room and Janie took the elevator up to the third floor and walked slowly down to the room where she had her baby girl. She never walked inside, never leaned close enough to see if anyone was in the room, but took a moment to stand at its threshold to say a silent prayer. She never lingered, not wanting to draw any attention.

After the hospital, she would walk through town out to the cemetery to visit her Mama's and Daddy's graves, making sure they were well kept, pulling out the scattered weeds, sometimes bringing a new flower from Kitty's garden to plant. Janie came to memorize the names on all of the surrounding gravestones, caring for the forgotten ones as well, as though their proximity in death made them a kind of family, too.

After she felt she had prayed sufficiently, knees bent on the hard graveyard dirt, she would walk down to the bar and have a cup of soup and a beer, saying hello to the now familiar faces, scribbling her address and phone number down, encouraging people to make the trip to Philadelphia, to come and stay with her and her sister. Janie recognized their looks of desperation. Mine jobs were drying up. Her town, more than ever, was becoming a place to leave behind. They shared their stories with Janie, husbands drunk and out of work, lovers lost, babies sick, sometimes nothing more than the sadness of a life just trickling by.

"Please come," Janie would repeat. "Please come see me."

So many did come, encouraged by Janie's kindness, by the promise of work, escape. Two sisters who were distant cousins of her Mama's came. They stayed on three years, living on the third floor of the massive house, William helping to put them through nursing school. Aunt Annie, who wasn't really their aunt of course, came and stayed a year, teaching all the children to curse and smoke during her extended visit. When Maggie would come raging up the stairs to catch them, Aunt Annie taught them to hide the butts in the hollow space within the statue of the Blessed Mother that she kept at her bedside. There were seemingly busloads of weekend visitors, always bearing gifts, homemade fudge, entire pots of soup held the two straight hours on the bus, lebanon bologna, sauerkraut.

Monday morning one or two often lingered, their distinctive upstate lilt floating up the stairs. Sarah would put them to work in the kitchen. Sometimes Kitty would find a way to cast them as an extra in her latest production. Maggie watched each visitor hawkishly, remaining detached, fully in control of her household. In time, stories of Maggie's and William's generosity made their way back upstate and in her absence, Maggie was forgiven. Janie, the self appointed messenger, was the only one who continued to return to their hometown.

On one of her visits back, there was a man—just once. Janie would not forget him. At first, she had ignored his offer to buy her a drink, stunned that he had chosen to talk to her. When she didn't answer, he came and sat next to her and politely asked again. She nodded her head in quiet agreement. He started talking. He wasn't from there, had only happened upon the tiny bar by chance. He was on his way to Scranton for a sales conference. He sold furniture to elementary schools, tiny chairs and desks, bookcases. He told her he had a catalogue in the car she could see if she wanted. He bought her a rum and coke, something she had never had before. She liked the sweet coke and even more the slow dullness that took over her senses from the rum, reminiscent of just waking up after a long night's sleep, peaceful, only half way present. She was on her third when she realized she was drunk. The bartender glared at the man, which thrilled her. His name was Bobby, a little boy's name she thought, a man with a little boy's name selling furniture for small children. It seemed so sweetly safe.

He asked her if she wanted to get some dinner. She went into the ladies' room and brushed her hair, lingering for a moment to look at her face. She was flushed, in a nice kind of way. When she came back, he took her arm and led her out to his car, his hand placed gently on her elbow, guiding her down the narrow street.

They never went to dinner. They parked in a lot behind the abandoned shoe factory. She had, ever so briefly, felt a rush of desire, before he took her, moved her hands, then her body, so mechanically, familiarly, that she began to cry before it was even over. When he was done he reached over to open the glove compartment to get her a tissue. Janie saw a picture of a little girl tossed inside, the corner creased and folded. She was dressed in a yellow dress with blue stitching, holding a fake sunflower.

"She's about the same age as my daughter is now," Janie said softly. He reached over and closed the glove compartment quickly.

He drove her to the bus stop and gave her twenty dollars. She took the money.

She would like to think that she was the kind of woman who would never go back to that bar again, but she did, ashamed of her disappointment when he never reappeared.

There are all types of longing.

The bus ride home was her last chance to daydream, to pretend, to imagine a different life. Only then would she allow herself to ask how it could have been different, to ask what if, what if she had locked her arms around her daughter that day and said simply, "She's mine. She's my daughter to keep."

The sight of the station always hurt because she knew it was time to put away this fantasy, to swallow her dreams down deep so that she could breathe again, so that she could carry on.

She liked to see the children before bed. They always plied her with questions about upstate, as though it were a mythical place, full of secret underground coal paths, harboring hidden treasure.

Kitty always left a book out for Janie on Thursday morning for the bus ride and Sarah always had a bag packed with a sandwich and something sweet. As soon as Janie walked out the door on Thursday morning, Sarah would close her eyes and look towards the heavens.

"Take care of her Lord—she is one of yours."

43

Maggie's hip held a baby effortlessly, her body naturally swaying to a calming rhythm. Each baby found a place there for a while and then relinquished it unwillingly as another one came to take its place. When William closed his eyes and thought of Maggie as he often did, he always saw her like this, her long dark hair ending where the baby's chin rested, her beautiful shoulders holding the small, plump face, one hand curved around the baby's bottom, one hand free, setting order.

He adored his children. He had never spent much time around children before his own. When Maggie had their first baby, Bonnie, he was terrified, mostly by the swell of emotion inside of him at the sight of her perfect face. He was happy to have so many women in the house climbing over one another to take care of his daughter, happy to only have to hold her briefly in his arms before someone would come and take her away. He didn't want to do her any harm.

But Bonnie wouldn't let him love her from afar, wouldn't let him care for her from a distance, like he was accustomed to doing. As soon as she could, she reached for him whenever he walked in the door. When she learned to crawl it was in his direction, to walk, she reached for his hand to lead him outside or to her books. He had no choice but to love her with every tiny piece of his soul.

When the second baby came, Charlotte, he was prepared to not love her as much, prepared to stay loyal to Bonnie, but she broke him too, as each successive baby would do. He learned that even he had a limitless ability to love his own children.

Once he took the three girls, Charlotte, Anne, and Bonnie, to the circus by himself. Maggie seemed uneasy, but she said nothing, dressed them beautifully and watched from the window as they left in his big car. They were enthralled from the moment they saw the big tent. He bought everything that came their way, the silver guns that shot colorful sparks, the cotton candy, the circus hats, the toy elephants. Twice his eyes filled with tears watching their faces, their pure, unpolluted joy. He wished to remember this moment forever, the circus lights casting an ethereal glow over his daughters' three enchanted faces. And then from Bonnie, a mild comment, nothing more than a child's wish, and it all changed.

"I wish we could see this forever, like it was in our own backyard Daddy, and we could help take care of the elephants and the little dogs that dance! Don't you wish that too, Daddy?"

He felt the familiar heaviness return. He could not make this last forever. He could not make their happiness last forever. There was nothing he could do to protect them, his girls. He was reminded of the story of Achilles, one of the many myths Kitty read to him as a child. Achilles' mother, Thetis, was immortal, but she'd given birth to a mortal son. She had loved her son so much that she sought a way to protect him, to make him as invincible as the gods. She carried her baby to the river Styx, holding fast to his tiny heel, to make sure he would not slip away in the dark waters. So tightly did she hold onto to her baby for fear of losing him, that one small spot remained untouched by the magic water, the mark where her immortal fingers pressed into her baby's flesh. Every other part of her boy was invincible, and yet danger found that weak spot, found her baby boy's heel. Achilles was to die when a spear found the place where his mother's fingertips had held him so tight, desperate to keep him safe, fearful that he would slip, that the river would take him from her first. And yet, she had lost her son anyway.

His girls would feel pain. They might even carry the very demons coursing through his own veins. He could hold as tightly as humanly possible, but he could not keep them safe from harm.

Maggie met them at the door that night. He could tell by her face that she had been anxious to let him take the girls on his own. She didn't trust him with her babies. He looked at his beautiful girls, tumbled together asleep in the backseat, their faces still sticky with pink cotton candy, their hands still clutching the night's treasures. He did not trust himself to keep them safe. Maggie silently relieved William of the weight of each sleeping child, placing them securely in their beds.

Over the years, William developed his own rituals, his own ways of protecting his children. Walking outside into the garden before dawn, he would repeat each of their names three times, facing once to the East and once to the West. At night before he could sleep, he would imagine each of their faces in excruciating detail. Though he could never bring himself to again enter, every day when he arrived at work, he would stand in the threshold of the hospital chapel and repeat their names once more.

Those who wait for madness to come endure a particular type of torture. They never know if their worry, their paranoia, is real or imagined. Were his worries about his children the same of any loving, responsible father or were they the beginnings of the same sickness that took his own father, that drove him to leave this world? These thoughts alone were enough to create a secret kind of crazy.

William could not bring himself to discipline the children. Maggie alone had that role. He feared that if he ever raised his voice, or got angry with them, a Pandora's box of evils would escape from his soul. Maggie seemed to somehow sense his weakness. She never asked him to step in, even when the boys were older. She had Kitty and Sarah and Janie to help her keep order, to soothe the tears once she meted out a punishment. William never questioned her judgment, grateful to have someone who was so steady, so clear.

None of them expected anything more from William, placing

him high on a pedestal because of his work, because of the life he provided. He sometimes wondered though if he reminded Maggie of her own father, if he shared the same weakness. He wondered if her father had drunk so much because he knew he could do no better for his girls, could find no way to shield them from the world, particularly a motherless one. He wished he had not judged the man so harshly in life.

Maggie's last delivery, her sixth, was difficult. The baby was breech and they needed to perform an emergency cesarean. William had a glimpse of what it might be like to lose her that night, to lose the mother of his children, to lose the one person he trusted to keep them all safe. He had a vasectomy the next day. There would be no more babies to love.

44

The little girl, Janie's girl, waiting at the bus stop pretended not to see him watching. She imagined the reasons why he couldn't talk to her, why he kept his distance, never fully revealing his face. She had seen him before. She pushed her hands deep into her wool pockets, trying to see him out of the corner of her eye. She would not draw attention to him by looking, especially while her mother watched so closely from the window. When she turned ten, the little girl insisted on walking to the bus stop alone, hugging her mother goodbye only in the privacy of their home. Still her mother would not relinquish her vigil by the window, her face tight with worry, her eyes ever vigilant.

In her adopted parents' story, her mother was very young, unable to care for a child and so she asked for a loving mommy and daddy to take care of her baby forever. There was no mention of a father. But the little girl has her own version of what happened, imagined countless times, every night before bed and in stolen moments of solitude. Her past has become this story, the one she has willed to be true.

In hers, her mother, a foreign princess had been killed by a rival, but not before quickly hiding her sleeping baby safely under the bed where no one would think to look. Her father, the prince, heartbroken, had found his murdered wife and assumed his baby girl lost until she let out a cry from beneath the royal canopy bed. Her father wept tears of joy and sadness. Knowing that she would never be safe from his enemies, he found a kind childless couple in America to raise her as their own, making them swear that they would never reveal her true identity. She had been delivered to her new parents wrapped in a blanket, the blanket her mother had swaddled her in moments before her death. It was the little girl's most precious possession. At night she buried her face in its careful stitches, certain that there remained a trace of her true mother's scent. Only death could have kept her mother from finding her now. This was her story.

He was forced to keep his distance. He watched over her as best he could, in secret. He longed to take her in his arms, to tell her he was sorry.

She fought the urge to look at him, to offer a slight wave, a smile. She loved him enough to keep his secret, to keep him safe. Like her mother, the princess, she would be brave. This would be her sacrifice.

45

Maggie watched her children run down the slate steps, ties loosened, carelessly carrying backpacks, Jeffrey swinging his violin, so at home amidst the golden haired boys and girls spilling out of the regal stone building. The plaque out front reads *Alcoate Friends 1887*. Maggie could not help but stiffen every time she walked through the front doors, hit with the intoxicating smell of privilege. Polished floors, leftover sand from St. Bart's, the soap from the country club bathroom, pressed sheets, tennis balls, all mixed together to create a magical elixir her own children somehow soaked up, absorbed completely. Yes, they were her babies, yet none of them held even a hint of her past, of the distinct, enveloping smell of her childhood, of poverty, of motherlessness. It was a smell that got inside you, became part of who you were, something she always had to remember to disguise. Even now, years later, standing here in the shadow of her children's private school, sycamores lining the drive, wrapped in her mink coat, sprinkled slightly with perfume, even now she worried about that smell, how it could still somehow escape, reveal.

Maggie attended every school play, dance recital, holiday event, always finding the perpetually empty seat next to the same woman, whose regal air and immaculate clothes could not disguise her shaking hands, nor the subtle scent of gin. The other women, the other mothers, were so removed from their houses, their kitchens, their babies, their men. William's prominence and money had granted Maggie a few invitations, but it soon became abundantly clear that she was not one of their own. These women spent their days dressing to go out to lunch, arriving to talk about nothing. Part of her knew that she avoided them because of Janie, too. She did not mind their loosely veiled questions about where she came from, how she met William, but she could not stand to see them question Janie this way.

Maggie would find her house full of their children, particularly the girls, longing for the attention and warmth that surrounded her own with so many women in the house, Kitty hugging every creature that walked through the door, Sarah insisting on feeding everyone, Janie memorizing everyone's names. Maggie was left to manage chaos, unable to escape the feeling that while their parents found it ok for her to feed their children, they would not come to the door for a cup of coffee, content to remain strangers. Had these children, children of the elite, been in coal country with mothers that stayed out all day lingering over drinks and lunch, never putting a child to bed or a meal on the table, and daddies who came and went like ghosts, people would shake their heads in disgust. But neglect seemed to be a privilege earned by the rich.

Maggie marveled at her children, how something that shared her blood could be so at home in this world of privilege. The distance from the Patch to the front door of their school might as well have been a million miles. Her memories of the past started to seem dreamlike, almost imaginary at times. When they were small, Maggie would fill the beautiful claw foot tub, one of six in her big house, testing the water to make sure it wasn't too hot for her babies who tumbled naked at her side, Janie helping to undress their perfect bodies. She remembered her mama heating water on the stove for their bath, a simple tin tub on the floor by the kitchen. Did Janie remember that, too? She would never ask.

Maggie would watch them, her children, afraid of her joy, of her overwhelming love, acutely feeling the fragility of every moment, waiting for the world to do them harm, as though tragedy was their birthright.

Ann was ten when she asked.

"Why don't you ever tell me stories about your mother?"

"What?"

"Your mother. You never told us anything about her. How come Janie remembers so much and you were the big sister? How come she remembers?"

"What did Janie tell you?"

"That your mother was so beautiful. That she had hair like you. That she could sing a million songs. Janie told me how your mother died. About your baby sister. That must have been so sad."

"What did she say? How did she say my mother died?"

"She said she died of a broken heart."

"That's not true," Maggie said sharply. "She got sick. A broken heart never killed anyone. That's a made up story."

"Janie said so."

"She is wrong. Now go on and get dressed."

Kitty had been washing dishes in the sink. She waited until Ann left to speak up.

"I'd have to disagree with you there. I believe a lot people die from a broken heart."

"I don't," Maggie answered quickly.

"You know—not everyone heals. There is nothing to be ashamed about."

Maggie spoke to Kitty in a voice she knew Kitty hadn't heard before, barely hiding the tremble in her speech, "I don't want my children to think that if things go wrong you can just give up. I don't want them to think the world can do that to them, that anyone can do that to them." Silently she repeated, *I will not lose them like that, I will not lose them.*

Maggie knew her words were pointed. "You should know. It's not fair to the people you leave behind."

Kitty took a moment before she answered. Her words were spoken to the window, the shadow of the theater visible in the morning light. "Maggie, loving something so much that losing it almost kills you doesn't make you weak. It takes a lot of strength to love that much, to let yourself love someone that much... and then to let yourself love again."

"I don't agree and I'd appreciate if you don't tell my children otherwise. That might be okay in your Romeo and Juliet but not in this world, the real world, the one I have to raise them in, the one they are going to have to live in on their own."

Kitty closed her eyes and turned away as she spoke, "Maggie—your children's lives—they belong to them. You can't decide what happens. Sooner or later you are going to have to realize that—every mother does. You can't direct their lives, you can't stop..."

"Kitty I'm not the only one directing. And at least I'm not acting, not pretending things are one way when we all know they're not."

"Really?" Kitty answered.

Janie walked into the kitchen taking in the tense silence.

"What's going on?"

"Ann told me you told her mama died of a broken heart. I wish you hadn't done that because it's not true. I don't want her to think something like that could ever kill you."

Janie looked down. "That's my story to tell, Maggie. You can tell her another one if you want, but that's my story. That's the one I am going to tell because it's true."

Maggie tried to make the words stop from coming, but she couldn't, "She's not your daughter. She's mine." She walked out of the room.

46

When the children were little, Maggie and Janie would wake them in groups, first the boys, then the girls. For so many years it seemed there was the changing of diapers, the heating of bottles, faces washed, clothes buttoned.

After everyone had been fed, Maggie and Janie used to take them with them on their errands, sometimes leaving one or two behind with Kitty and Sarah. For years there were strollers, then tightly clasped, small chubby hands. The children would scramble to hold onto Janie's instead of Maggie's.

"You squeeze too tight," Bonnie used to say, pulling away from her mother.

"If you paid attention and didn't try to run I wouldn't have to pull so hard," Maggie answered.

Bonnie was undeterred, "Janie doesn't pull me. She holds my hand soft," locking her dark eyes with her mother's, her jaw set in an identical line of determination. Maggie was the first to look away. Bonnie always ran ahead grabbing for Janie's hand, Maggie feeling the familiar sting of resentment made worse when Janie would nudge the little girl back towards her mother, softly whispering, "Hold your mother's hand—be a good girl."

Bonnie would walk back reluctantly, obediently reaching up for

Maggie's hand. She would yank it firmly to her side, mortified by her own jealousy.

With each passing year, school took another one of them, until one day Janie and Maggie found themselves alone, holding on to only each other as they crossed the street. At each stoplight, Janie would reach for Maggie's arm, finding the tender spot left behind from Maggie's break as a girl. Maggie would pull her arm back, annoyed, but Janie could not break the habit of reaching out for her sister's hand, of trying to steer her towards safety.

"The days are long, the years are short," Kitty would recite. Maggie would roll her eyes. But it was true. They were growing up. There were new fears, dangers, mistakes to anticipate. Janie would find her sister sitting up at night in the kitchen, waiting for one of the children, teenagers now, to come home. Maggie would be pressing gently on that tender spot on her arm, just like she did when she was twelve.

"Maggie, she's okay," Janie would offer softly. "Don't worry—she'll be home soon. She's a good girl."

Maggie would say nothing. Janie would pour them a beer to share and they would sit and play cards in silence. Later, Maggie would remember these moments as the closest they came to their old life, two girls sitting together trying to keep fear at bay, waiting for someone to come home.

Maggie would jump up when the flash of headlights gratefully shone in the kitchen window. In would come one of the girls, flushed with a night of young love, or loss.

"You're late. I have been sitting here worried sick," Maggie could not contain her own fear.

"I'm ten minutes late—please relax."

"Don't tell me to relax..."

"Janie—can you please talk to her!" the girls would shout in exasperation.

"She is not your mother. I am. I make the rules here. Not Janie. Go to bed," she would hiss, disgusted by the sound of her own voice.

Maggie could feel the anger pulsing inside of her, the unfairness of it all, her sister, Kitty, Sarah, her husband too, all of them but Maggie, allowed to purely love her children, free of the constant pressure of keeping them safe.

Janie spoke softly from the table, "Maggie—let it go—it's ok... she's safe, safe and home. She's here now. Don't fight with her."

Maggie stood with her back to her sister when she spoke, "You don't understand do you? You can never understand."

47

The tiny bird rests on the branch of the holly tree having wandered far from the creek bed. Janie is standing at her bedroom window, letting her eyes linger on William, her sister's husband, as he wanders the yard, quietly pausing at times to make some unknown calculation, observation. His hair has just begun to show slight flecks of grey at the base of his neck, his sideburns. He fingers the forsythia bud, on the edge of bloom.

It was her Daddy who showed her this bird first. "Kingfisher," he used to point, speaking in hushed tones. "Spends half his life waiting, just watching the water run by."

Sometimes they would hear its song first, walking the path until they spotted its pointed black beak and the gentle silhouette of its grey and white body perched on a branch stretched over the water. They would walk into the woods on Sundays, after church, their Mama having gone quiet after weathering another Saturday of Daddy's drinking. Desperate to escape his own guilt and the suffocating silence of their mother, he would head to the woods. Maggie never went with them, choosing to stay behind with Mama, her own type of silent protest. This was before they lost their baby sister, before Mama's eyes went dark, vacant, when she could still feel rage, when she could still feel anything at all.

"Kingfisher," Janie repeats softly, now watching Michael, Maggie's youngest, just seven, asleep in her bed.

Michael had woken her up during the night. A nightmare he'd said. He'd tapped her gently and she'd moved over to make room for his small, warm body. He smelled like summer, a subtle, salty heat radiating from his skin.

"You okay Michael? You feel okay," she had asked sleepily reaching for his forehead to test for fever.

"Janie?"

"What is it, sweetheart?"

"I don't want you to leave," he nestled in closer.

Janie opened her eyes, "Why do you say that? I'm not leaving. I'm not going anywhere," she whispered lightly, uneasily. She leaned her face into his hair, still damp from his bath. He was quiet.

"Promise?"

"I'm not going anywhere. I won't leave you. I promise."

She'd watched as his forehead relaxed, how he'd let out one long deep breath before giving in to sleep. She had memorized this moment in each child, the marking of when they passed from awake to dreaming. She could not fall back to sleep herself, watching as dawn came, carefully climbing out of bed when she heard the back door slam, marking William's start to the day.

William methodically checked the feeders every morning, each one requiring a special seed to draw in a different type of bird, cardinals, woodpeckers, chickadees, yellow finches, warblers, sugar water for the hummingbirds, gently working the suet down the wire to stop the squirrels. He reminded her then of Father Timothy, the father of her child, a memory that filled her with an uncomfortable, misplaced desire and yet, she could not take her eyes from the window. As the first light approached, the tiny birds came to wait knowingly, such small wondrous creatures, grateful for the seed, incapable of judgment.

Janie was in the kitchen when William walked in from outside. They were always the first ones awake. They had their own quiet routine, William placing the papers on the kitchen table, Janie making his coffee, keeping it hot until he came inside, exchanging only the smallest pleasantries, sitting together reading the paper while the rest of the house began to stir, the day still new.

"Good morning, Janie," William said softly.

"Coffee?"

"Please. You okay, Janie? You look a little tired."

"Michael had a bad dream last night—he came into my room around two a.m. I couldn't fall back to sleep."

"Did he say what he dreamt of?"

Janie laughed uncomfortably. "He said he dreamt that I left. Little angel made me promise that I wouldn't leave."

William was quiet for a moment.

"Janie?"

She looked up.

"I don't know what we would do without you... Any of us. We need you here. I feel like you are part of this family—I can't imagine life otherwise..."

She felt the rush of warmth inside of her as he spoke, as he held her eyes so gently.

Kitty walked in singing. William looked quickly away.

48

A thousand fears have disappeared with each year, and yet heartbreak still finds them. Her children take their secrets, take their tears to Janie. Maggie hears their hushed voices on her way up the stairs. They have chosen her sister to tell their stories to. She cannot stop her rage, her face crimson as she hears only the urgency in their whispers, she cannot stem the feeling that something has been taken from her, stolen unjustly. But then, whenever there is a school show, an award given, or a picture taken, Janie retreats into the shadows.

"They are your children," Janie insists. "You go and be proud." Maggie cannot bring herself to demand that her sister share these occasions, remaining silent.

She feels her own cruelty acutely, knowing that each milestone pierces Janie's heart even more than her own. Her sister lets herself grow sad at the passing of time, recalling first words, curls lost, favorite toys. Maggie refuses, determined to see each passing year as a gift, as though looking back, allowing any type of regret or longing, will leave her vulnerable to loss.

"They are getting so big so fast," Janie laments, seeing them off to their first day of kindergarten, middle school, graduations.

"Janie, stop your tears. They are alive and healthy. This is a celebration," Maggie repeats.

The children know Janie will listen to their mistakes: the pursuit of the boy who was no good, the party where they'd had too much to drink, their envy of another. They know, too, what Maggie will tell them to do and that she will be right, that there will be no argument. Maggie will tell them to walk away, to never let themselves become too attached, too dependent, to look to the future, to trust no one but themselves.

Maggie knows it is the same with William. One night she awakes and finds their bed empty. She goes to the window to see if his car is still in the driveway. She doesn't remember a middle of the night phone call from the hospital. His car had not moved.

She walks downstairs and begins to check on the children, room by room. She finds Janie's bed empty.

She will never remember why she led herself down to the basement, or even why she walked so quietly, careful not to be heard. She knew neither of them to be capable of infidelity, infidelity to her at least.

But when she finds them sitting side by side, not touching, while William holds his head in hands crying softly, part of her feels as betrayed as if she had found them in the midst of passion. She knows there are things they will not tell her, are afraid to tell her. Like the children, perhaps her husband knows that she will not stand for weakness. He might have even believed that Maggie would not love him in his weakness. He might have been right.

49

*T*ime swallows you up, first teeth, first steps, first words, first day of school, lost teeth, learning to ride a bike, haircuts, heartbreak. The days are endless taking care of so many, keeping so many safe from harm. Your memories stay jumbled except for your mistakes, you will remember your mistakes. They are babies reaching up with fat fingers, and you coax them to walk, each day a step further. Later you will watch your baby boy, just five, fall from the top of the slide, certain that he is broken beyond repair. You will watch your sister reach your baby first, wipe away the gushing blood to reveal the wound.

"He is ok," she will repeat calmly while you still stand paralyzed, unable to touch your boy, images of his lifeless body scattering in your mind. You see him twisted, covered in coal dust.

He will need three stitches. Michael touches the scar gently while he sleeps, as though it is still tender.

Your daughter Charlotte is singing. It is your mother's song. How does she know the words? She sits cross-legged on the thick oriental rug in the paneled living room whose grandeur still stuns you. She is twelve, tiny hints of womanhood appearing on her slender frame. Her voice is your mother's. You want to tell her that, you want to take her into your arms, push back the loose strand of dark hair that falls across her face, teach her the words to all the songs that you still remember. You want *to tell her of this miracle, but you stand too long in the doorway. Your mother's face appears to you. She is not singing, but rocking, her lips dry, cracked, her hands clutching air, still reaching for what is lost. You turn away from her song.*

Bonnie is toddling across the kitchen floor in her blue smock dress. She is light itself, her laughter filling the room. One day she will stop smiling. You will not hear her laugh, laugh the way you remember, for two years. You will never know why. You are afraid to ask. She is twenty now.

You wake in the middle of the night still even though they are no longer babies. You hear their phantom cries. You wander from room to room, even sitting on the neatly made beds of the girls, who are gone, gone off to college.

At this hour you remember what it is like to love them, how it is all that matters, how you need to tell them that every day. You promise yourself it will be that simple. You will love them, nothing more.

But when morning comes it is different. There is breakfast uneaten, the eggs untouched on the plate. The promised phone call that never comes. There are the menacing eyes of the men on the corner as they see your girls walk by. There is the unfinished homework on the stairs, the fever that appears at midnight. You cannot afford to be distracted by your love.

They do not love you like they love your sister. This you will remember.

You cannot escape the feeling that you have misplaced something, left something behind. It follows you everywhere, a steady ache of anxiety. You feel memories slipping further and further away. You dream that one of the children is lost, that you cannot call them back, all the while knowing that they are wandering towards darkness, towards danger. Your voice fails you again and again. Someone is missing. You awake with your throat dry, your husband's side of the bed still empty. Have you found the life you wanted?

50

Kitty sat at the kitchen table peeling the potatoes in silence. Sarah was at the stove. She looked up and saw Janie walking towards the house from the garden. She was singing. Sarah could see her mouth forming the words but she could not hear the song through the glass.

When Janie opened the door to walk inside, there was a rushing sound, as though she had just let in the rain. It was a bird, a female cardinal, it wings beating frantically as it tried to find the open sky. It had followed Janie inside.

"A bird! Janie a bird just flew in behind you!" Maggie laughed. "Watch out here it comes!"

"Open the door! Poor thing is going to kill itself!"

Janie stood still and watched the bird fly, stood motionless, while it circled the room and finally found a path out the open door.

"Janie, you okay? Janie?" Kitty asked.

"I'm fine. Funny—I didn't even see it follow me inside."

Kitty's Daddy had told her that Cherokee blood ran through her veins, that although it was just a drop, remnants of an illicit romance, it was enough for Kitty to see signs. She chose to believe this story.

She knew a bird in the house meant death was coming. She knew the bird had followed Janie in. She caught Sarah's eye. She knew Sarah knew, too.

That night Sarah excused herself early from supper. When Kitty found her later to ask if she was okay she said, "There were some prayers I needed to say. I haven't been to church in some twenty years, but today I felt called to pray."

Kitty understood.

51

The next week, Janie didn't come down for breakfast in the morning. "Where's Janie?" Kitty asked when Maggie walked into the kitchen.

"She's not down yet?" Maggie answered surprised.

"I'll go up and see her," said Sarah.

Sarah came back down a few minutes later.

"Female problems," she whispered to Kitty and Maggie. "I'm going to make her some tea."

"I'll take it up to her," Maggie said, frightened by the uneasiness in her stomach.

Maggie knocked softly on the door to Janie's bedroom. She realized she hadn't been in her sister's room in ages. She felt awkward, as though she were entering a stranger's room. Countless times she had walked by to hear the children laughing or stood in the doorway and watched one of her children sleeping close to her sister. It was their domain, not hers. Janie was still in bed, her face turned towards the window where the bird feeders hung outside.

"Janie? You awake?"

"Yeah—sorry I didn't make it down. Did the boys get off to school okay?" Janie went to sit up.

"Yeah—normal groaning."

"Did Michael remember to take those papers for the field trip? I left them on the counter."

"He took them. I brought you some tea. Are you okay?"

"Oh yeah—I'm sure I'm fine. Just been having some heavy periods—they seem to wipe me out lately. I'm just tired."

"Are you sure? Do you want me to make you an appointment? I could run you down today?"

"Oh no. I'll be fine. Just need a little rest that's all. I'll be fine. I'm sorry I'm just worthless in bed up here."

"It's okay—you should sleep—do you need anything?"

"I'm okay—thanks Maggie."

Maggie walked out.

The next day Janie was down as usual.

It went on like this for a while. Maggie would later realize it went on like this for months. Who knew how many mornings Janie didn't complain? A week would go by and then Janie would sleep in one day, Maggie, Kitty, and Sarah, checking in on her, bringing her tea, lamenting what women have to go through each month. Janie always seemed to be better the next day.

Finally one night, after the boys had been put to bed, Janie came to see Maggie.

"Maggie?"

"Yeah—come on in."

Maggie was in her bed alone reading the paper, William still at the hospital.

Janie came and sat shyly down on the edge of her bed. "I've been thinking that maybe I better go see someone, someone at the hospital. I'm sure it's nothing, but William recommended someone there. Would you mind driving me to the appointment tomorrow? It's at 9:30."

"You told William?" Maggie asked startled that Janie would talk about something so personal, so female with her husband.

"Well, yes I did, the other day. He asked me how I had been feeling. I guess I've been staying up in bed enough for him to take notice—I usually am the first one down in the kitchen with him in the morning," Janie blushed.

"Oh. Okay. Sure I'll drop the boys off at school and then I'll take you. You are okay though?"

"I'm fine. Just better get it checked out... So is Charlotte going to be back from school for her birthday? I was thinking about what to get her. I think she needs a new raincoat. The last time she was home she told me she had a tear in the sleeve of her other one—that light blue one she had that looks so pretty on her?"

"Yes. She said she'll be home."

And then there was a new topic, Janie ever so clever at drawing the attention away from herself.

The doctor's appointment turned into a follow up appointment the next week. That turned into an overnight stay in the hospital for observation, tests.

Maggie could feel the panic rising inside of her at each piece of news.

"Why does Janie have to stay at the hospital tonight?" Michael asked.

"They just need to do some tests."

"Is she okay?"

"She's fine. She'll be home tomorrow."

Kitty waited until Michael left the kitchen.

"Do you really think she's okay?" her question piercing Maggie in a thousand places.

"Yes. I think she's fine. Female problems—they just have to figure it out. Ask your son," she answered tersely.

Sarah said nothing.

Maggie picked Janie up at the hospital the next day.

Janie waited until they were in the car to tell her.

"They told me they need to do a hysterectomy. Need to take everything out they said."

Maggie gripped the steering wheel, took a breath, "I'm so sorry, Janie."

"It's okay. I'm not having any babies anyway," she laughed awkwardly. *Anymore*, she thought silently.

They were quiet for a while.

"But they said after the hysterectomy everything will be okay? Right?" Maggie asked again.

"Sure. Sometimes the recovery takes a little while, but I should be fine, just fine. I think I'll feel tired for a while—but that will nothing new, right? William promised he would be in the operating room throughout the procedure. That was nice."

"Yes, good," Maggie could only answer once again stunned at the degree of intimacy her husband had with her sister.

It was scheduled for a Monday morning. That day Maggie took Janie to the hospital planning to wait, but Janie hurried her home, saying she knew they would take care of her, William was there to make sure everything was okay. Maggie wasn't needed there.

"I'd feel better if you went home, Maggie. I wouldn't want the boys to worry."

"Janie, I don't mind staying," Maggie had said unable to say, "I want to stay with you."

"Please... The girls come home this weekend, too—you have to get everything ready for them."

Maggie nodded yes.

"I'm so glad they're only keeping me a few days...that I'll be home in time for Charlotte's birthday. I can't wait to see them...I feel like it has been so long since we've all been together. Go on now, Maggie—it's already past noon—go home. I'm fine."

"Ok then. I'll see you tomorrow. Call me if you need anything else."

"I will... don't worry."

Maggie drove home, surprised by the warm tears that gathered on her cheeks, the fear that beat in her heart.

Maggie had waited all day to hear from William. Every time the phone rang she jumped, but he never called. She couldn't sit still. She threw herself into getting everything ready for when Janie came back home. She made up her bed with new sheets and pillows. They were beautiful with hand-stitched robins on the shams. She and Sarah spent the better part of the day scrubbing down every surface. Kitty arrived with three vases full of flowers, seashells collected by the children to line the windowsills, and a stack of books. Maggie walked in while she was arranging them on the shelf.

Kitty looked up, "We just started this one. It's one of my favorites, *The Secret Garden*. Janie loves it—says it makes her want to work all day in the garden. I think too, she relates to the little girl—she lost her mother like you girls did. For the first time, we are both taking turns reading out loud. It's taken twenty years, twenty years of stories and encouragement, and finally, I think your sister is not embarrassed to read in front of me. I've heard her, in her room, read to the children before, bedtime stories, but never for me. It makes me so mad when I think about it, what Janie must have had to go through in school to carry such shame with her still. She is so bright, she's doing so well—she's reading so well. She just needed some time. There will be a whole world opened up to her now, a whole world of stories."

Maggie was silent.

"Did William call yet?" Kitty asked.

"Not yet," Maggie answered.

"He'll call soon. Don't you think? He'll call?" Kitty asked, looking for reassurance.

"Yes, soon," Maggie answered.

Janie was supposed to come home. She was supposed to let them take care of her, to heal, to read the books that lined the shelf, to marvel over the drawings Michael had left at her bedside, to call them in to see the woodpecker, to take her place again at the kitchen table, stirring her tea, laughing, eager to hear their every story. Janie was supposed to come back to them. She was the mother that Maggie couldn't be. They needed her—all of them.

William never called. Maggie decided this meant that everything went as planned. She could not bring herself to pick up the phone.

He came in late that night, after Kitty and Sarah had finally gone to bed, Maggie hurrying them out of the kitchen, eager to be alone to wait for news. She was restless, organizing the drawer of forks and spoons, the multitude of teacups and saucers. She jumped when she heard him come in.

He walked to the window first, keeping his face away from her, resting his hands on the radiator, peering out into the blackness where his bird-feeders hung, silent and lifeless in the dark.

"Maggie..."

"You're home... good," she could not look at him, keeping her eyes locked on the stack of saucers, her hands busy. She would not let him deliver bad news.

He walked closely to her side as if to embrace her but stopped short, "We've got to talk about Janie."

"I know. I know we have to talk about her. I was going to pick her up Wednesday morning after I drop the boys at school. Do you think they will release her by noon?"

"Maggie, look at me." She looked up. His face was red with grief, still marked by tears. "They're not going to release her."

Maggie was silent, waiting, frozen.

William picked up the blue china dish that sat on the table where Janie placed her tea bag every morning. Sarah had put it there. It was waiting for her.

"I am so sorry."

"Why are you sorry?" Maggie could feel the familiar panic in her stomach. It may have been almost forty years ago, but she would never forget what true fear felt like. In a moment she was back in the Patch, watching her Daddy shuffle back and forth on the porch, trying not to look at her and Janie, coming to tell them something about their new baby sister, and later, something about their Mama.

"Janie is real sick. It wasn't what we thought. We were wrong. She has cancer. She's had cancer for a long time now. When we opened her up it was everywhere. It's in her liver, her bladder, probably her lungs too by now."

"What are you going to do? When is she coming home?"

"She's not coming home. Janie doesn't want to come back here. She doesn't want to put the children through that. She wants us to send her upstate as soon as we can. She wants to go home."

"Home? This is her home. Why would you let her go upstate when she is already in the best hospital? When you work here? When you can make sure that she gets the right care? I don't understand?"

"Janie wants to go..."

"Who cares what she wants? You are a doctor—you know the best treatment is here. You have to tell her that she has to stay! If it were your sister, if you had a sister, or if it was Kitty or Sarah, or one of the children you wouldn't do this, you wouldn't let them go! You would do anything you could to keep them here, to save them..."

"We're not trying to save her..."

The slap came quickly. It was the only time Maggie had ever struck another person. William, lightly touching his cheek, hung his head, and continued to speak quietly.

"They will take good care of her upstate. It's what Janie wants. It is her choice. I am so sorry that I couldn't help her, Maggie, that I can't make her better."

William had continued to hold the blue china dish, gently cupping it in his hands. He placed it now gingerly on the kitchen table, as if his touch alone could render it into shattered pieces. He left Maggie in the kitchen, knowing that if he tried to embrace her now he would find her stiff in his arms.

Maggie sat in the kitchen alone, her body cold, her hands pale, as though life had already begun to seep from her as well. She forced herself to climb the stairs to the guest room. She would not sleep next to William tonight. The door to Sarah's room was ajar. She could see Sarah and Kitty holding each other, rocking with their sobs, trying to stifle their sounds of suffering so as not to wake the sleeping boys.

Outside of Kitty's room, on a high table, stood a marble replica of Michelangelo's statue of David, purchased on a family trip to Italy. Kitty had guided them through the country, grabbing her grandchildren's hands in Piazza Navona to marvel at Bernini's Four Rivers fountain, ran her hands across the intricate brick work of the Coliseum, stood with tears in her eyes underneath the miracle of the Sistine Chapel.

In Florence, they looked up together at Michelangelo's David, the beautiful young boy on the verge of slaying the giant for his people, his perfect figure sprung from a block of marble by the artist's hands.

"What do you think, Maggie?" Kitty had asked her daughter-in-law.

"I guess I'm not an artist," Maggie had replied.

"Oh Maggie... we are all artists. It's what makes us human, our longing for beauty, despite the suffering, the ugliness in this world. We write songs, poetry, plays, we paint—even find the figure of beautiful young man in nothing more than a left behind piece of marble. It's what separates us from the animals. It gives me hope when I see this kind of beauty—hope for humankind."

"Like I said, I guess I'm not an artist."

Kitty answered softly, eyes still fixed on the looming statue, "I don't know about that. I've seen the way you make a bottle for a baby, the way you iron their little clothes, make their beds up with fresh sheets, braid the girls' hair. There is beauty in that, too. That too is a kind of art."

Maggie had said nothing, eager to gather her children to her in the crowded museum, resentful that William and Janie and Sarah were still lingering at the base of the giant boy, heads tilted upwards, eyes filled with wonder. Maggie called to her children sharply, knowing it was up to her alone to make sure no one got lost, especially here, a million miles from their home.

She stood in the hallway before the model of the statue now, fighting the urge to knock it off the table with her fist, to watch young David smash to pieces, his heavy stone weapon rendered useless. She wanted to call into Kitty that her collection of beautiful objects had meant nothing, had done nothing to disguise the fact that the Earth was a place of suffering, full of loss.

Their sobs awoke a pit of anger inside of her, "She is my little sister!" she wanted to scream. "Mine to keep safe!"

But Maggie hadn't kept Janie safe. Her years of prayer, of imagining every disaster that could befall her children, their father, her surefire method of preventing grief by envisioning it in its most graphic detail, all of these efforts had forgotten Janie. Tragedy had come to her, found her weak spot, pierced her completely. The world was going to take her sister because Maggie had never even once imagined losing her.

The weeks that followed were like a dream. Maggie, gathering the children in her room, having rehearsed her speech countless times, telling them that Janie was sick, that she wasn't going to get better, that she wasn't coming home. She didn't recognize the depth of her own grief until she saw it on the faces of her children, until she heard the sobs that came from deep within each of them, cries that she had not heard from her babies ever before, sounds that remind us that we are animals, that sorrow is physical pain. She was lost.

And then, the weird giddiness of the ensuing weeks. Janie had insisted that Maggie bring the children to see her one more time in the hospital upstate before she felt too sick, before she looked too sick. She greeted them with smiles, so alive, so much their Janie, that they forgot their fear, and Maggie for one, began to hope, to believe despite what everyone had told her that this really would not be the end. Janie acted like a tour guide from her hospital perch insisting that Maggie take them to see what was left of the old house, the long since shuttered mine, Mama and Daddy's grave.

Everywhere they went, people knew who they were. These people took Maggie's children into their arms, invited them into their houses, insisting on giving them food, a beer, a cup of tea. Maggie looked at her beautiful children. They had traveled all over the world. Once she had stood and marveled at their faces from atop the Eiffel tower. Another time, on a cruise to San Juan, William, having had too much to drink, had hired a man to take them to the bioluminescent bay. All of them, Janie too, huddled in a rickety boat with outstretched hands, splashing through the water, tossing up magical blue sparks into the air, leaving behind a brilliant brief imprint on the dark water below. Maggie had stopped for a minute to watch as her children and William splashed, captivated by the glitter of their movements, the wild magic of the water surrounding them, echoing with their shrieks of pure joy and laughter. As the warm drops bounced off her skin, her heart surged with longing, an emotion she could not explain. She was surrounded by everyone she loved, but at that moment she recognized the particular ache of homesickness.

Now she understood. When she looked at her children, she saw glimpses of the faces of these people. How could she have not seen this before? All her years of trying to get away, to finally realize that what she was most proud of in her life was being from this place. It was why she didn't mind the exclusion of the other mothers, the other wives, why when the school called her in to tell her that William Jr. wasn't able to stay, that it wasn't the right "fit" for him, she was able to stand up and say, "In my day they called it dumb. There is no shame in being dumb. The most shameful acts I have ever witnessed have been at the hands of intelligent men. William is a good boy. He will be a good man. Thank you," leaving them speechless at what they mistakenly perceived as her own ignorance. But Maggie knew better. She had wondered at her absence of shame, her lack of interest in being accepted. It was because she had come from here, from this place, where decency was the only currency that mattered.

They say that the stone uncovered by strip mining for coal will sometimes reveal the fossil of an ancient fern, our earliest plant. Maggie would always think of this when she saw the ferns come alive in spring, their green vitality connected to the deepest past. Such were the faces of her children and the people surrounding them now.

The day they left, they stopped finally at her parents' graves. Her children surrounded her, so much life, so much joy, gathered here at her parents' final resting place. They would have marveled to see them, her children, their grandchildren, their strength, their confidence, so capable in the wide world outside of this tiny Patch. But Maggie knew that if her father appeared to her now, taking in her beautiful family, his eyes would stay searching and he would ask one single question, *Where is Janie? Where is your sister Janie?* And Maggie would have to tell him that she hadn't kept her safe.

Maggie answered her children's questions with the detachment of a historian until Bonnie came and unexpectedly hugged her, close enough to feel the pulsing sobs that Maggie kept locked inside.

"It's okay, Mama," Bonnie repeated. "It's okay to be sad. It's okay."

Maggie let her daughter, a woman now, hold her. She could say no more.

They walked down from the hill together. Maggie knowing that a space had been left open for Janie to join them at last.

They went to the hospital to say goodbye. Janie called them all in at once and kept them so busy with questions and laughter. They each stopped to hug her in succession, reassured that they would see her again, that she was still full of life. Janie wouldn't leave them yet. Maggie, comforted, told her sister she would be back next week. Janie smiled and shook her head yes.

"Michael?" Janie called the youngest back into the room. Maggie started to walk back in with him.

"Can I have a minute to talk to him alone? Do you mind?"

"No—not at all. I'll wait outside."

Michael came to her side of the bed. His face had started to thin, beginning the transformation from little boy to young man.

"I wanted to tell you a story. Just a short one. You know my mother, your grandmother, died when I was still a little girl. I haven't seen her face or been in the same room with her for over thirty years. Now you might not believe me, but I have met her many times since. My mother is out there... sometimes in the way a perfect stranger smiles, or sometimes in the voice of a little girl singing, sometimes during a rainstorm, I just know she's there. It doesn't matter where you are, I will find you... Will you look for me? Will you help your brothers and sisters and Kitty and Sarah and your daddy and... and your mother, will you help them find me, too? Because I will be there."

Michael nodded, burying his head on Janie's lap.

"Now go on before your mother thinks I'm telling you where I hid my money!!"

Janie waited until she knew they were safely out of the room and down the hallway before she let herself cry. She knew she would never see them again. She had tried to memorize each of their faces as she hugged them goodbye, to take in each of their different smells as they buried their heads in her shoulders. They were her babies, too. She loved them so much. Alice came and quietly sat by the bed. Janie began to speak softly through her tears, at last unleashed.

"I feel like I've spent my whole life saying good bye to people I love. I look at them and I want to see them again. I'm so tired of saying goodbye. You know one time I was in a room down the hall sitting with a young miner. Right before he died, he looked out the window and he told me he saw fairies, fairies tapping on the glass. I thought that was so beautiful. Do you know what heaven would look like for me? Looking through the glass and seeing all of them, my baby girl, Maggie's children, all the people I have loved, watching them safely through the glass."

52

The priest, Father Timothy, was no longer a young man. He could feel old age approaching despite the absence of its usual markers. There were no wedding anniversaries to celebrate, no children's birthdays to mark, no home holding fading photographs or memories.

He had continued to make mistakes, mistakes that could not be hidden, that could not be forgiven. He had learned to remain silent about the mistakes he saw others make. The powers that be lectured him on being more cautious, prescribed prayer, then sent him somewhere new, leaving his shameful acts behind for others to silently remember. Each new place was poorer than the last, the faces in the pews darker, places where the constant lurking presence of unpunished, authorized evil was expected. They sent him to these places to preach the word of God.

They kept moving him until he landed here, as far from their gilded chambers as he could travel, here to Africa, to a mission in Rwanda.

He would awake each night underneath his mosquito netting, listening to the sounds of the jungle outside his guarded bungalow. He was never without a guard, sometimes two, dutifully watching the pale white man, dripping with sweat, whose mere presence was supposed to bring hope, help, perhaps even salvation. He was never alone, never away from eyes of the village people who did not want him to die on their watch. At last he felt safe. He would do no more harm.

The heat left him weak. Aside from suffering through the daily mass he did nothing, taking tea on his porch, his collar as always more powerful than a superhero's cape. The people took pains to shield him from the very sorrow he was sent to relieve.

He was delighted by the rare birds, the sounds of gorillas calling in the distance, the impossibly beautiful, impossibly lush landscape that was Africa. For the first time he believed there truly might be a God. How else to explain the dazzling blue of passing starlings or the way heaven itself seemed to descend every morning over the lake, briefly captured by the verdant crest of trees until the sun took its place, burning off what could only be described as celestial mist? He had never known such beauty.

Would he remember Janie's face? They had had a child together. At one time, in his longing, he had memorized the exposed stretch of skin from her chin to the tender crevice at the base of her neck. Would he remember her voice if he heard it again? Would he remember any of their voices?

53

If Maggie woke up and the feeder outside Janie's window was full of chickadees it sometimes meant that Janie was going to get better. A single yellow finch meant she would not. The butcher handing her back three golden pennies, looking her in the eye and saying God bless you and your children gave her hope. She monitored her every action, her every thought, feeling like each one could alter the outcome of her sister's fate.

She drove back upstate three days after the children had visited.

Janie had been moved to a different room. Maggie panicked as she stared at the empty room, the freshly made bed, but Alice called from down the hall and led her down to Janie's new room.

Janie was ashen. Maggie bit through her tongue to suppress her tears, her shock. It was as if Janie had used up all her life in her last visit with the children. Maggie could feel death coming. She had seen enough people die to know what it smelled like, what it looked like, when you couldn't run from it anymore. Janie reached over and took Maggie's hand. Maggie squeezed back. Janie knew enough to not pretend anymore. They were silent for a while. Janie spoke first.

"It was in this room here that I said goodbye to my baby. She was a little girl, Maggie, lots of hair like Mama's baby. Sometimes, Maggie, I wish I knew her name, so when I pray for her, I could say her name out loud. It would be nice to hear it, to know it belonged to her, even if it wasn't a name I'd left for her."

Maggie took a deep breath and prepared herself to finally listen to her sister's story. She nodded in encouragement for Janie to go on.

"You know what the worst part is, Maggie? She knew I was her Mama. I know she went with a wonderful family, but when I held her for those few minutes before they took her away, she knew—she knew I was her Mama and she was glad to see me, glad to be in my arms. I know you probably think I'm crazy talking like this about a tiny baby but it's true. Do you know what hurts the most? What keeps me up at night? That she missed me that day. I think about the people from the hospital taking her to some family, a good family, Dr. Baker promised me that, but still I think she knew she wasn't with her Mama. When I picture her little arms reaching out and her perfect lips looking for my breast, her nose trying to find my smell, even if it was for one day, for one hour, for one minute, I think that little baby missed me and I will never forgive myself for putting her through that. Do you think she could have loved me? Do you think I could have been a good mother for her?"

"Janie, you were 15 years old..."

"Maggie, I know what I was. Answer my question—please tell me, you're the only person I can ask."

Maggie looked at her sister, suddenly small in the hospital bed. Countless images of her own babies crawling into her sister's lap rushed into her head—Janie wiping their tears, holding fast to their tiny hands, rocking their perfect bodies slowly by the window in the middle of the night. Finally Maggie answered, "I think she would have loved you with every ounce of her being and yes, you would have been a good mother, a great one—better than most... better than me."

"I was afraid you were going to say that."

54

Maggie heard the phone ring in the dark and she knew at once. Janie had died, a mere six hours after she had hurried Maggie home, hurried Maggie once again away from her pain, away from her loss, and Maggie had listened, Maggie had gone.

They had taken her body already to the funeral director's, flesh to ash as quickly as they could per Janie's orders. Maggie was left to weep at the door to the open room, unaware that she stood in the holiest place in her sister's life, that her sister's feet had stood there countless times, praying for her daughter. Alice came and found her. They held each other in the doorway and wept together openly, two middle-aged women, heartbroken. They had been waiting for death, knew it was coming, but perhaps death's cruelest trick is no matter how loudly it approaches, its final arrival still leaves one utterly stunned. How could Janie really be gone?

Maggie had spent her life, after her mother died, waiting for more loss, grabbing hands of children on busy street corners, pulling them away from the oncoming trolley, blocking them from the loose dog on the corner, cutting their food into smaller pieces, staying up all night to watch their fever, lifting them up from the waves at the beach, ushering out the boyfriends with greed in their eyes, locking the front and back doors at night. She had been vigilant.

She had done everything she could for her children. She had resented Janie's confidence, always declaring that they would be okay, that Maggie should have more faith, more faith in her children.

"Let them run!" Janie would say as Maggie tried to keep them close on the way home from the store. Maggie fought the urge to cry out, as her children pulled away from her, leaned towards Janie and her promise of freedom, fought the urge to scream, "You have already lost your child!" She knew this would only be heard as madness. She could not stop her belief that the world was waiting to take one from her. It was her turn.

Maggie had kept her children safe, but grief had gotten her anyway. Janie was dead. Maggie had never seen it coming.

Alice had a box at her house of the few belongings Janie had brought with her to the hospital. She told Maggie she would keep it safe for her until she was ready to come and pick it up.

Janie had planned meticulously for everything. Her headstone, the flowers, the hymns, the prayers, even the dinner to follow in the back room of a tiny neighborhood bar, where the owner let Maggie know that Janie had asked for extra mashed potatoes for the children.

Janie knew Maggie would be lost, knew she would not be able to make any of these decisions on her own. She had taken care of her.

During the service, Maggie was startled to see William rise and walk to the front of the church. He began to sing *Amazing Grace*. His voice filled the tired old space, making the song seem as if it was written for them alone.

When he came and sat beside Maggie he caught her eye.

"She asked me to," he said softly.

As the trail of mourners snaked on, Maggie began to embrace each face, certain that even those unfamiliar to her would make themselves known. She loved them all for coming for her Janie.

A man about her age approached, his face so strikingly familiar that it took her breath away.

"God Bless, Janie. Your sister had a heart of gold. She is with the angels, of that I'm certain."

"Joseph," was all she could say before he had moved on.

Maggie resisted the urge to call him back, to run after him and take him into her arms. He was the last one who would remember her Janie as a girl, remember her like Maggie did. She wanted to run away with him and make him talk for hours, make him repeat every story, every memory that held her Janie. But she had broken his heart and even now, so many years later, could not ask him to help heal her own.

55

Joseph walked quickly from the church, freshly shaken by being near Maggie once again. "You're a goddamn fool," he said aloud to no one as he marched away, brushing the sweat from his forehead, clenching his hands into tight fists, breathing deeply to expel the still familiar smell of her from his consciousness. After so many years, how could the sight of this woman unnerve him so deeply? He had been seventeen.

Though he never married, Joseph was always in the company of women. Finding other women, anyone but Maggie, came easily.

He was convinced that if he could slice himself open wide he would still be able to see the scar, the damage she had left behind, not just in his heart, but in every cavity of his whole being. She was just a young girl, he shouldn't have expected anything more, but he knows he was never the same. When she left, when she let that other man touch her, everything changed.

He had done well for himself. He had a house. He had become the fire boss in the mine. He was considered by all a decent man, especially after Maggie left him and he still stayed loyal to her family, loyal to Janie. After that, he could do no wrong.

Joseph had prayed for a noble death after she left, prayed for the mine walls to close in on him, for the chance at rescuing others if only he could be left behind. But no harm would come to him, almost as if Maggie's complete evisceration had left him somehow invincible.

He had imagined seeing her again, once he heard about Janie. He knew she would come back this time. He had thought endlessly about what he would say to her, certain that he could hurt her too in her moment of grief with the right, well chosen words. But instead he had said nothing, nothing except trite prayers for Janie who deserved so much more, words spoken only to drown out the single question he found himself suddenly aching to ask.

Will you come back?

56

The children had gone home with William. Maggie told them she would get on the road in a few hours, that she needed to take care of a few things before she left.

She drove slowly to Alice's, memories surging back at every corner, the houses lining the road like mourning soldiers. So many of the places in the Patch now stood empty. The coal company took what they could then up and left. In their wake came the Kmarts and McDonalds, empty storefronts on Main Street, young people gone. The hollowed out hills stood like ghosts on the town's rim. You could pay a dollar now to ride the coal car into the mine, like it was some kind of roller coaster.

Alice looked out the window as Maggie climbed the porch. She had been waiting.

"Good to see you, Maggie."

"You too, Alice."

Maggie came in and took a seat at the table. She put the bag she was carrying down.

"I brought you some of Janie's sweaters." She reached in and pulled out a neatly folded pile. "I gave each of the girls one, too... She was always cold, even when we were little. I know she would have liked for you to have some of them. They're good, warm sweaters."

Alice lifted the pile from Maggie's arms. She could smell Janie's scent tangled up in the wool.

"Thank you, Maggie. They're beautiful... Come and sit ... tea?" Maggie nodded. Alice went and fixed her a cup. Maggie waited silently at her table, taking in the tidy room. Alice came back in with a tray and sat down.

"How you doing?"

Maggie said nothing for a while. Alice waited patiently for her answer. "I know I just watched them bury my sister, but I still can't believe she's gone. I can't believe that she died the way she did. I can't believe I'm here and she's not. I pray a lot now—I thought it might help, but all I seem to ask God is why he gave her all the bad luck and me all the good? Why? It's not fair."

"Life's not like that, Maggie. It's not one big pie getting divvied up. Janie didn't think it was like that either. She loved you and she loved your children. She didn't blame you for getting to keep yours. She loved them."

Alice stood up and got a box that she had set by the door.

"These are just a few of her things she brought to the hospital. I packed them up for you. She told me she wanted you to have them. Afterwards."

Maggie reached in and pulled out a small photo book. In it were all of her children's school photos, neatly arranged in order. Maggie could recall Janie sitting at the booth in the kitchen carefully dividing the row of pictures for William, Kitty, Sarah. She had kept a set each year for herself.

Maggie reached into the box again. She pulled out the Dr. Spock baby care book. She turned it on its spine to see Mahanoy Public Library. She looked up at Alice curiously.

Alice answered softly, "She wanted to know about babies, taking care of children, after she had her little girl. She wanted to know how she was growing every year, when she would learn to talk, walk, how she should have been taking care of her, if she hadn't given her away. I think it helped her to feel in some way like she was a part of her life."

Maggie could only nod, the constant sob that lurked in her chest threatening to escape again. When she opened up the book, out fell the chain of paper dolls. Maggie carefully picked them up.

"I don't remember these. Do you know what these are? Why she kept them?" Maggie asked.

Alice said nothing but looked at the row of featureless faces. Janie had left them behind knowing that Maggie would get this book, would discover their yellowed faces carefully tucked inside. Alice felt compelled to tell their story.

"Maggie, the father of Janie's baby was a priest... one of our priests."

Maggie looked up wild-eyed. "Who? What priest? I don't remember any priest?"

"Do you remember the young man who was here for just a few months while Janie had that job cleaning the priests' home? Father Timothy?"

Maggie searched her mind. His face came back to her in shadows, a stranger.

She felt the rage surge inside of her, "Did he know? Did he know what he had done?"

Alice nodded yes. "Janie found that in his bible. She took it with her. She kept it because she believed it showed that he had some goodness inside of him, despite what they did, what he did. She said she needed to believe that her baby's Daddy had some good in his soul, too. She said whenever she looked at that she felt better because only a man with some heart would carry with him a fading chain of paper dolls."

Maggie ran her finger over the ancient paper, her rage transforming into sadness, "She never said a word... I always thought it was just some boy coming to see her in that empty house after I left. I never imagined it was him, anyone like that... Did my Daddy know?"

"No. Nobody knew. Nobody would have done anything anyway."

"Father Timothy..." Maggie repeated his name. "Thank you, Alice, for telling me. It matters to me that I know what happened now. And thank you for being so good to Janie."

"It helped me, too. It helped me to have her as a friend. Another mother who..." her voice broke into sobs.

Maggie handed her a tissue and took her hand. They sat like that together for a while.

Maggie got back on the road by dark, the paper dolls tucked back neatly in the pages of the baby book.

57

Maggie wore her navy blue suit, pearls, and the emerald ring William had given her, absurd in its enormity. She was well aware of what money could buy.

The church secretary greeted her warmly. William did not believe in God, refused to enter the Catholic Church, but did not stand in Maggie's way when she took his children. He knew better than to try his word against such power.

"So good to see you, Mrs. Lane. How can I help you today?"

"Nice to see you, too... As you know, my sister Janie passed away recently," the words still stuck in Maggie's throat. She fought the urge to simply say, "My sister is missing," so certain was she that she would come back, that Janie could not have possibly left her completely.

"I know. I am so very sorry. She is in my prayers."

"Thank you. I'm actually here today to ask for your help with a matter concerning my sister. In the town where we grew up, when we were much younger, there was a priest in our parish. He knew my sister. I know it was a long time ago, but I would like to get him a message, let him know about Janie since he was... so kind."

"Well of course. How can I help?"

"Like I said it was a long time ago. I only have the name of our parish and his name, Father Timothy, and the year he was there..."

The secretary cut him off, "He was only there a year?"

"Why yes. But you know how long a year can be in the life of a young girl? And we had lost our mother when we were so young— and so..."

"Oh yes—I am so sorry."

"Do you think it would be possible to try to find Father Timothy? So that I could get him a letter? A letter about my sister?"

"Well of course I will try. Sometimes places keep good records, sometimes not. But I'll see what I can do."

"Thank you so much. Please also let Father Frank know that we are more than happy to sponsor the women's luncheon."

"Wonderful. I'll be in touch soon."

It took only two weeks, two weeks to follow the path of his lifetime, to track him down. There are some things the church chooses to remember, to record.

"The church lady is on the phone!" Michael yelled.

Maggie picked up. "Hello?"

"Hello—Mrs. Lane?"

"Yes."

"I think I finally tracked down your Father Timothy. He is quite the world traveler!"

"Really?"

"Do you have a pen and paper? Because this address is a long one. He is at mission now, a mission in Africa! A place called Rwanda! That's gonna cost you a bundle in postage! Are you ready?"

"Go ahead," Maggie copied down the address, repeating it twice. "Thank you so much for your help. I am so appreciative."

"You're welcome. Also Father Frank wanted me to ask if you had any interest in helping out with the new Sunday school bibles?

"Of course. You can tell him that I'll drop the check off tomorrow."

"Thank you, Mrs. Lane. You are always so generous. I hope your letter finds this Father Timothy."

"Thank you. I hope so, too." Maggie hung up the phone.

58

Janie had been gone 54 days. Her smell still lingered ever so slightly on the chair she used to sit in by the window. Kitty kept the flowers fresh on her dresser. William kept the bird feeders full outside her window. Sarah could not bring herself to remove the saucer for her tea, still waiting on the table for her return home.

Maggie dug with her bare hands into the soil in front of Janie's headstone. She placed the Lily of the Valley plants gently in the shallow hole and patted down the soil firmly. She had driven upstate that morning, as soon as she saw the boys off to school, slipping out without talking to Sarah and Kitty, leaving behind a note that said only, "I'll be gone until dark."

Maggie was alone in the cemetery. She brushed her hands over her sister's headstone tenderly.

"I brought these for you, Janie. They are all over the garden this spring. The smell hits you when you walk out the back door. Every time I smell them I think of you. But then again, anytime I do anything I think of you. When I'm making soup, I wait for you to ask me if I added the onion. When I'm walking to the store, I wait for you to ask me to take the long route so you can walk by that house that has all those bird feeders out front so you can catch sight of a yellow finch. When I'm reading the paper in the morning, I wait for you to ask for the sports section. I miss you all the time. The children, they miss you so much. I find them crying in your bed in the middle of the day.

"Last week, Michael was praying to St. Anthony because he lost his library book. He told me that whenever you prayed to St. Anthony for something that he lost, he found it. Now I find myself saying that prayer out loud, like a crazy woman, praying for you, 'Dear St. Anthony please come round, Janie's lost and can't be found.' I keep saying it, over and over again. 'Please come round, please come round.' That's why I came up here today. I needed to see your gravestone, because I keep thinking you are going to come back to us, that I am going to look up and see you walk into the room.

"I look for you everywhere. I followed a woman from a distance in the grocery store the other day because she reminded me of you—I started to think that maybe you'd come back, come back to see me, to tell me something, like a visiting angel. Kitty told me to try to start each day remembering something good that we did together. She told me that if I work at remembering the good things, eventually they will outshine the bad memories. But I find myself wishing that I could do it all again Janie, differently. I wish I hadn't left you. I wish I had been there with you when you had your baby. I wish I had listened better to your stories about Mama instead of wishing you would stop talking about her for once because it hurt so badly. I wish I wasn't so afraid... afraid that... that my children would love you more than me—I felt like loving you meant they wouldn't love me as much—like there was only so much love to go around... I am so sorry.

"I tried so hard to forget about what it was like growing up, with Mama sick, and Daddy drinking, afraid all of the time of what was coming next that I forgot that the whole time I had you. You never left me. Even when I went away, you never left me. And now you're gone, and I don't know what to do. I don't want to get out of bed in the morning anymore. I can't believe that I am alive and you are dead—it's like I shouldn't be able to breathe on this earth without you here. I want to stay under the covers and I want to remember, I just want time to remember everything about you.

"But I can't stay there. William needs me, the children need me, Kitty needs me. There is no time in real life for true grief, for the endless tears that I want to cry for you, Janie. And I'm so scared, because I have to show my children how to live with this sadness, how to live with losing someone you love so much. But I don't know how—I don't want to learn how. I don't want to tell them that you are better off with God, or that you are in a happier place, I want to figure out how to get you back.

"I remember once I asked you if you really believed in miracles, in all those stories they told us in Sunday school. I remember what you said, you didn't skip a beat. You told me, 'Yes, I believe in miracles, I think they happen every day, all the time, everywhere.' And that's why I keep praying, praying to get you back, so that I can tell you how much I love you, how much I need you in my life. You are my sister. You are my baby sister. I don't want to be here without you... That's what I came here to say."

The sky was darkening, a line of deep pink marking the sun's departure, the distance between light and darkness. Maggie finally stood and left. Had she paused and looked behind her she would have seen a pair of ancient nuns, leaning on one another, slowly headed towards Janie's grave, carrying a wicker basket full of sweet William, eager to be planted.

Maggie wasn't ready to go home yet. She pulled her car in front of Davey's, the same bar where she'd heard William sing for the first time, transfixed, transformed. The inside was unchanged.

Maggie sat at the bar and ordered a beer.

"We have good soup today—navy bean—would you like a cup?"

"Sure, thank you."

Maggie ate the soup and ordered a second beer. It was 6:00. She knew she would have to leave soon so she could see the children before bed.

A woman walked in and sat at the bar and ordered a beer.

"How you doing, Paul?"

"Good, how about you, Patty?"

"Not so good. My mom's back in the hospital—another fall."

"Oh God love her—I'm so sorry to hear."

"She's a devil—won't listen to anything we tell her. Ninety-two and she's still trying to drive her own car!"

The woman quickly glanced down the bar at Maggie. She looked back again and let her eyes linger.

"Excuse me, you wouldn't happen to be Maggie Coyle would you?"

"Yes. Yes I am."

"It's me Patty, Patty Jones—I worked with you at the hospital for a while before I moved to Allentown."

"Oh my God, Patty—how are you? It's been over twenty years! You look good."

The two women talked, reminiscing about old stories, faces, rumors, instantly familiar with one another, comfortable.

Patty took another sip of her beer and tilted her head to the side.

"Maggie, I heard about your sister Janie. I'm so sorry. I didn't know her well, but she was a good soul."

"Thank you, " answered Maggie.

"I'll never forget the day she had her baby. I know it broke her heart to give that baby up. We saw a lot working at that hospital didn't we?"

"Yeah we did," said Maggie distractedly. She felt a cold weight inside her, making it hard to look up, to keep asking questions, even though she didn't know why. Here was someone who knew Janie, someone she should talk to, someone she should make remember.

Patty looked uncomfortable, seeing that the mention of Janie's baby made Maggie pause, look down. *We all have sad stories we try to forget,* Patty thought.

"I know my sister had a baby girl. I know she gave her away, Patty—don't worry—you're not spilling any secrets," said Maggie firmly. "I know about the baby," she repeated.

Patty seemed to relax at these words, comfortable that she was sharing only a memory with Maggie, a common story.

"She'd be a grown woman now, that baby," Maggie continued as if she was talking about the weather.

"Seems hard to believe doesn't it—time goes so fast. I still feel like I'm twenty even though the mirror and the scale tell me otherwise!" Patty laughed.

"How is your husband, Maggie?"

"He is the same man you remember. Always busy, always working hard, still hard to get a laugh out of," Maggie smiled. Patty nodded in agreement, recognition.

"I'll never forget driving down to Philadelphia with him that day. He was clutching the steering wheel, not saying a word while I was holding a screaming baby, neither of us having any idea what we were doing!" Patty shook her head, remembering.

"What baby?" the words escaped from Maggie's lips on their own.

Maggie watched as Patty froze, as fear replaced the lightness in her eyes. She waited, searching her mind for the right answer to give Maggie.

"Janie's baby," Patty said quietly. "I thought you said you knew?"

Maggie didn't move.

"I'm sure I'm not telling you anything you didn't already know am I?"

Maggie said nothing.

"I'm so sorry. Jesus, I'm not myself today. I've had so much going on with my mother. I'm not thinking clearly."

Maggie still could not speak.

"We were so young. We..." Patty fumbled for words, but there was no turning back. She was too tired to try to cover it up now, to try to weave a different tale. It was too late. When she finally spoke again, it was more to herself, then to Maggie, who sat locked in silence.

"We really did know how to keep a secret back then didn't we?

Now everyone tells everyone everything, but not when we were growing up. We kept our secrets locked up tight."

Maggie still had not spoken. Patty put a bill on the bar.

"This is on me. I've got to get going. God bless you and your family."

Maggie began to shake as she watched Patty leave.

She didn't remember the ride home. She quickly kissed the children goodnight and went and sat in the kitchen and waited, her shock transforming into anger.

William walked in exhausted, startled to see her and the light still on.

"Hi sweetheart, how was the trip back?" He bent to kiss her—she turned away.

Her words were full of hate. "You knew. You've always known. You knew where Janie's daughter was since the day I met you. You helped give away her baby and you never said a word."

William looked down, pausing before answering, as though his reply had been rehearsed countless times, mindful of each word, "It was what she wanted."

"You are talking about 1954. A fifteen-year-old girl, alone, having a baby out of wedlock, with no mother of her own. Did you ever think that she might have changed her mind? That she might have wanted to know that the man she was living with for the past twenty years had driven her baby girl to her new home?"

"I was told she didn't want to know. I was told to take the baby away. I was asked to help."

"To help? You think you helped. You think that by driving that baby down to Philadelphia she disappeared out of Janie's life and in your mind it was like you stitched up a wound—that in time it would heal, leaving behind just a thin scar thanks to your surgical ability. It's not like that—it never healed. She lived with that raw, jagged wound every day of her life. You are a heartless man. If I could have shown Janie her daughter once, it could have changed everything."

William eyes glazed over with anger. "For who? For you? Not for Janie. She still would have died and she still would have given that baby up. Maybe it would have changed things for you. Maybe you would have been left feeling a little less guilty for having abandoned your sister upstate so that you could pursue greener pastures. Maybe you could have felt like the hero bringing Janie back her long, lost daughter. Maybe then you would feel better about your mistakes when it comes to your sister. I love Janie and I miss her and I think about her all the time, too. I did what I thought was best. Did you? Did you ever once think about her baby? Because I do, all the time. Did you ever ask Janie if she changed her mind? Or what it was like to give her up? No, because you didn't want to know! You weren't there," William stood over Maggie. He had never before spoken to her with such rage. Maggie did not cower.

"You were wrong!" she seethed. "I am going to find her, I am going to find out where Janie's daughter is..." William cut her off.

"You want to find her? You want to find Janie's daughter? Go ahead. She works at Northeastern Hospital, obstetrics. Her name is Alice Philips. Her adopted parents were killed in a car accident three years ago," William stood to leave the room.

Maggie was momentarily silenced by this news. *Alice*, she thought, that would have made Janie so very happy. She knew what number bus went to Northeastern. She and Janie had ridden that bus together before. They might have passed by her daughter one day perhaps.

"She is my niece. I'm going to meet her, to tell her about her mother, about how she lived and about how she died, and that not a day went by that Janie didn't think of her and pray for her safekeeping. She deserves to know how much she was loved by the mother who gave her away."

William stood suddenly deflated, arms limp at his side, head down, eyes locked in on the waxed kitchen tiles. "Sometimes there is no way to fix your sadness. Sometimes you have to find a way to live with its constant company..."

He did what he thought was right. He followed the rules. He could hear his father's voice saying, "I don't know how to help you, I don't know how to help myself."

William wanted to tell Maggie that this was the crushing ache that awoke him in the middle of the night. The crying, a wail filled with such longing, screaming out in his head, that baby's voice mixed with the memory of his own desperate tears for his mother, that baby's plea to turn the car around, to take her home to her mama. He had understood. He knew what it was like to leave your mother when every instinct in your body told you that you should be with her, comforted in her arms. He remembered, but he didn't turn back, did he? He could have always turned back.

He would walk to the far end of the basement in their cavernous house and there he would sit with his head in his hands and let himself cry, cry until the sobbing quieted in his own head, until the ache felt a little lighter or until morning came. Once when he had been down there he had felt a sudden touch on his shoulder, he jumped to recover himself thinking it was Maggie or one of the children, but it was Janie.

"Is there anything I can do?"

"Afraid not, Janie. Please don't..."

She cut him off, "Everyone should be entitled to have some privacy in their grief. I imagine that a man like you would have to come all the way down here to be alone. But if you don't mind, I'd like to sit with you awhile."

"I don't mind at all."

"You're a good selfless man. You've got nothing to be ashamed of," Janie had said no more, but sat quietly with him until dawn.

But he was not a good man. He knew what made Janie wander down there in the middle of the night. He knew what memory haunted her perpetually. He wished he could have spoken up then, could have told her, but he had already made his choice, he had already done what he was told, without protest, without thought. He imagined the words coming out of his mouth. He imagined speaking up at last and telling Janie, "I know where she is Janie, your daughter. I was the one that drove her to her new parents. I was the one who took her away. I thought I was doing the right thing, I was told I was doing the right thing. I have watched her for you, Janie. I have made sure she is okay."

But it was too late. He, a young resident, was told by his attending doctor to drive the car, to drive the baby away from her young, poor mother, with no husband, no family to speak of except a battered old coal miner, shaking in the corner. He knew if he told Janie then, she would have asked about that car ride and he would have had to tell her, tell her about how her baby cried, how the nurse that held her could find no way to soothe her tears, that the memory of her baby's voice still wakes him in the middle of the night, that he has never heard a more desperate plea.

It wouldn't matter that he had driven by her house every day since they had come back to Philadelphia, watching her take toddling steps across the lush green lawn, laughing into her new mother's arms. It wouldn't matter that he had seen her warm in her winter coat, waiting on the bus stop. It wouldn't matter that her hair grew so long when she was a teenager, that she wore it back in one thick braid. Her adopted father was a doctor, traveled in the same circles as William, so it didn't take much to find out where she had gone to college and later to find out where she went to medical school. When her parents died in that terrible car accident, it was easy for him to make a phone call to recommend that she get the obstetrics residency, people were more than willing to accommodate his request to remain anonymous, to be discreet. It was easy to find a reason to visit the hospital where she worked, to see her in her white coat, a serious young woman.

I have watched her for you for years, the words wandering silently across his tongue.

But Janie would have wanted to start from the beginning, to start from the car ride away. His years of watching, of keeping vigil, would have meant nothing.

Finally William spoke again, "Finding this girl, this woman, isn't going to bring Janie back. It's not going to make you stop missing her. I am truly sorry."

"I have no choice," Maggie stood and left the room. She went and slept in Janie's old bed, too angry to cry.

But still, Maggie waited a month before doing anything, a month of again watching for signs.

It finally came to her in a dream.

She is underground, trapped in the mine, running. She is running through the blackness, climbing over rock, trying to find a way out. In the distance she sees a small glimmer of light. It is just a tiny opening but Maggie digs at the rock with her bare hands, clawing through the blackness, digs until she can climb out. When she finally escapes it is night. She is in an open field, a million stars scattered across the sky. She keeps running until she sees a small fire in the distance. She runs until she gets there and she sees a tiny figure curled up, seemingly lifeless, on the edge of the fire, glowing with smoldering coal. I am too late she thinks, too late. Maggie takes the creature into her arms and pulls back the small blanket covering its face. She unveils four-year-old Janie, laughing, smiling, shouting out, "You found me, Maggie, you found me!" In the dream Maggie presses her face into Janie's hair saying the words repeatedly, "I found you, I found you." She wakes up still saying these words. She climbs out of bed to the window. She swears she can smell coal smoke in her hair, on her skin, her hands.

59

The sun had risen to its highest point, encouraging both man and beast to slumber. Father Timothy had just risen from his chair off the porch to go inside and rest when he saw the boy running up the road waving the letter.

"Father! Father! Father!" he shouted.

He was breathless when he reached him, small beads of sweat glistening off his round, dark forehead, triumphant. The watchman came and snatched the letter from him, insisting on handing it to Father Timothy himself. The boy, forlorn, stepped away, but still he waited. It was the first letter Father Timothy had received in his five years at the mission. It was not lost on the boy that this was an occasion. There was no return address but the postage showed it had come from America. Father Timothy could tell it was a woman who had written his name by the way the letters curved. That much he had not forgotten.

He stood on the edge of the porch and began to carefully open the letter. As he did, the single row of paper dolls escaped from the envelope, the wind taking them quickly, blowing them off the front porch of his bungalow and down the path. Father Timothy could only stand motionless with the envelope in his hands, his arms outstretched.

The village boy ran after the floating paper figures, capturing them gently. With cupped hands he ran back, gleefully repeating a single phrase over and over again. He smiled wondrously as he placed the fragile paper in Father Timothy's hands, still clutching the envelope, a neatly folded letter still tucked safely inside.

"Umumarayika! Umumarayika!"

"What is he saying?" Father Timothy asked the watchman.

"Angels, Father. He is saying that someone has sent you angels."

The envelope in his hands tugged in the wind.

60

Dear Father,

My sister's name was Jane Coyle. She was the mother of your child. At fifteen, she gave birth to a baby girl, your daughter. She gave her up and never saw her again. That baby is a woman now.

I do not expect you to remember my sister. I do not expect you to mourn the loss of your daughter. I do not expect you, a so-called man of God, to feel at all.

You did not ruin my sister. The fifteen-year-old girl that you abandoned who gave up her only child was not destroyed by you.

She was loved by so many people. By all my babies. By my husband. By his family. By countless others she showed kindness to, expecting nothing in return.

You took so much, but you could not touch her spirit, her goodness.

My sister is dead.

She would have forgiven you. Perhaps your God will, too. I will not.

Margaret Coyle

61

The hospital floor was quiet. The familiar hospital smell, the constant attempt to mask the odors of the sick, the dying, with starched sheets, bleached floors, sent a flood of memories back to Maggie. Odd that this smell could remind her of falling in love, of watching for William on every hallway and yet also remind her that her sister was dead. A woman about Maggie's age sat at the reception desk, eyes fixed on a stack of charts.

"Excuse me?" Maggie began, not recognizing the sound of her own voice.

"Yes," the woman looked up coldly.

"I am looking for Alice Philips. She works here."

"You mean Dr. Philips?"

Maggie stopped herself from saying, "No, I'm looking for a girl..." pausing briefly before replying, "Yes, Dr. Philips."

"What is this regarding?"

"I knew her family. I would have contacted her at home, but I didn't know her home address."

The woman looked at her skeptically, annoyed.

"My husband is a surgeon. He is acquainted with Dr. Philips. He suggested that I come here to talk to her. I understand how busy doctors are."

The woman's demeanor changed completely, "Of course. You can have a seat. I'll page her."

Maggie sat down to wait, trying to calm her beating heart. Janie's baby girl was a doctor. The woman had called her Dr. Philips. She delivered babies. She caught life in her hands every day.

She knew it was her when she saw her approaching, pacing quickly down the hallway. She had her thick, dark hair tied up in a neat ponytail and when she looked up at Maggie, she saw Janie's eyes, Janie's freckles, spilled across beautiful full lips, Bonnie's lips.

Had Maggie remembered more, she would have seen also Father Timothy's daughter, the pale, nervous parish priest, only dimly present in her memory due to his insignificance in her own life. But she had never bothered to truly observe this quiet man on Sundays while he fumbled through his sermon. Maggie had spent Sunday mornings restless in the hard wooden pew, contemplating the stained glass windows, anxious to be released, to distance herself from the sister who prayed so fervently by her side. Father Timothy had meant nothing to her and she had been utterly blind to her sister's devotion.

Alice had inherited the deep dimple in Father Timothy's left cheek. The tiny pieces of his fractured heart remained his alone to carry.

"Can I help you?" their daughter Alice asked.

"Yes, I'm Mrs. Lane, I mean Maggie. I apologize for showing up at your work like this, but it was the only way I could get in touch with you. I knew your family and I need to talk to you."

Alice sat down and began to speak calmly, detached. "I'm sorry if you're hearing this for the first time, but my parents were both killed in a car accident two years ago this January."

Maggie looked into her eyes, Janie's eyes, "I knew your birth mother. She was my sister. She died."

I know my mother is dead. She was a princess. The childishness of this imaginary story occurring to Alice with devastating swiftness. She silently repeated the locked away, long forgotten story she had told herself for years, *My father is a prince, he used to watch over me. Only death would have kept my mother from me. Only death...* Such foolishness.

Maggie waited for this young woman in front of her to react to such news, but instead she said crisply, "I'm leaving here at five o'clock. There is a diner around the corner. I need to get back to work now but if you'd like, I'll meet you there then."

"Thank you. Yes... I'll be there."

That was in two hours. Maggie decided to wait. She sat silently on a bench outside the hospital until quarter of and then she walked to the diner and took a seat and ordered a coffee.

Janie's daughter arrived shortly.

The waitress asked her if she would like anything and she quickly shook her head no.

"So..."

"So, thank you for coming. I guess you are wondering why I am here, why I contacted you now after all these years. You see—your mother, my sister, she died—recently."

"I'm sorry."

Maggie found herself shaking, the words tumbling out awkwardly, "I guess I wanted you to know that your mother was a really good person and that she loved you and prayed for you every day. I wanted you to know that if you ever have any questions, or if you would like to see a picture of her, I live close by. I thought you might want to know that. Here is my number and my address."

"Thank you. My parents were very open with me and I knew that my mother had had me when she was very young. They always told me they would help me find her if I needed to, but frankly I never felt the need to. I'm so sorry for your loss."

They sat silently together for a while.

"Do you have children? Are you married?" Maggie finally asked.

"No—no children, not married."

"I'm sorry I don't know why I asked that—it's none of my business."

"It's okay. Lots of people ask me that," she laughed lightly and Maggie felt stricken with the sudden similarity to Janie. She remembered that laugh, a quiet chuckle, forced from within, meant to put you at ease—how had that laugh traveled all this way?

"Well, I guess that is really all I came to say," Maggie said softly.

"Well... thank you."

She stood and insisted on paying for Maggie's coffee. They walked out together.

"Where are you parked?" Alice asked.

"Oh, I took the bus," replied Maggie.

"I'll walk you to your stop."

This woman, Janie's daughter, was a stranger, still lost to her now. They walked to the corner and started to cross, but an approaching car made an unexpected turn in their path. Alice reacted quickly, reaching out for Maggie's arm to pull her back, her fingers finding the tender spot on Maggie's wrist, the same spot where Janie's fingers always came to rest when she reached out for Maggie. This time though, Maggie didn't pull away.

Once the car had passed, Alice continued to hold onto Maggie's arm, guiding her across the street. By the time they got to the other side, Maggie wept openly, while Alice held her, hushing her softly, like a mother.

"I loved your mother so much, but I left her, I let her have you all by herself. She was fifteen. I wasn't there to hold her hand, to tell her everything was going to be ok, like she did for me. I didn't know, I didn't know what it was like until I had my own baby, your cousin, Bonnie. You look like her, the same beautiful mouth, the same dark hair. When I had Bonnie, I took one look at her beautiful hair and eyes and fingers and I knew then. I knew what it must have been like to give you up, to put you in the arms of a stranger and to say goodbye. I used to watch your mother with my own children—here I went and had six—and she loved them so much. Every day I know she thought of you, what you were doing, what you were like, how she could have ever let you go. And I never asked. I was too afraid or maybe too ashamed. I never asked your mother about you.

"You were the last person she talked about. The last thing she ever told me was about loving you. I miss her so much. Every day, every moment, everywhere I go, I miss her, I carry her with me everywhere. Everything I see, everything I do, I think about how she isn't seeing it, too, how it would be different if she were here. Now I understand what it is like to lose a part of yourself. And maybe my husband was right when he said that I came to find you for myself, for a way to make myself feel better, but I did think that if you knew how much you were loved and prayed for throughout your life that that might be a gift that I could give to you from your mother, a gift she couldn't give to you herself."

Alice took Maggie again by the arm.

"Do you mind walking?" said Alice.

"No, not at all."

"Why don't we take a walk and you can tell me about your sister, about my mother?"

And that was the beginning.

Some people might say that it was a coincidence that the car had appeared at that moment, that Alice had only happened to reach for Maggie's arm, accidentally finding the tender spot left behind from that break so many years ago. But Maggie chose to believe that it was her sister Janie, reaching out to her from the heavens, reaching out through her baby daughter to grab onto Maggie, to help her find the words she so desperately needed to say. Some people might have said it was luck. Maggie chose to believe it was something else.

Acknowledgements

I want to thank John Hassett, my former Spanish professor at Swarthmore College, and his beautiful, brilliant wife Elizabeth Subercaseaux for reading the first fifteen pages of this book and telling me to write more. Without your kindness and encouragement, this story might have stayed in my desk drawer in the same Spiderman folder forever. Thank you, John, also for being such a faithful reader of chapters and for your insightful comments and edits. Thank you to my friend Dana Calvo who took the time to read my first attempts at this novel in the midst of her own busy writing career and who has always encouraged me to keep writing despite setbacks.

To my sister Robin, an amazing writer, who was the first family member I was brave enough to share this with since so many memories conjured in the story are close to our hearts. To my brother Gavin for getting me my very first copyright and always having my back. To my sister Kim for being an example of someone who always keeps art alive in her own life. To my brother Bryan who connected me with the wonderful people at Deeds and who is already encouraging me to write the next one.

To the amazing women who took time out of their busy lives to read this story: Angela Shaw, in addition to being such a wonderful friend thank you for being the one who taught me about the kingfisher at just the right time; Vicky Huestis, for sharing the Roosevelt quote and countless other books and articles and for the positive emails that I'm certain could pull me out of even the darkest abyss; Diana Campbell, for taking the time to give such helpful feedback and for knowing what this book was really about before I did; Carlin McCoy, for keeping my first draft in a fireproof box; Dana Reinhardt, Reisa Mukamal, Mary McCabe, Jean Steinke, Donna Painter, and Abby Finney.

To Monica Schadlow and Emily Reichman, my college roommates, who miraculously still love and support me despite knowing everything about me. Victor Hugo said, "laughter is the sun that drives winter from the human face," so it with us. I am so grateful we found each other—how did we? I'm certain none of us remember.

To my children: John, whose own beautiful writing inspires me. Ava who would have never, ever, accepted anything less than the publication of this book. Rowe who showed her encouragement by banging on the office door and asking, "Seriously how long does it take to write a book?" and Anthony, my business advisor in all matters. And finally to my husband, John, one of the hardest working men on the planet, who has always made me feel like I can do anything I set my mind to—truly without you there would be no story.

I am the great granddaughter of a Pennsylvania coal miner. His daughter, my grandmother, and her kindness and resilience inspired me to write this story. Thank you Nana.

About the Author

Katie Crawford is a 1993 graduate of Swarthmore College. She taught public elementary school in both Philadelphia and Swarthmore for nine years following graduation. She currently resides in Swarthmore with her husband, John, and their four children, John, Ava, Rowe, and Anthony. When not staring at the screen and figuring out what to write next, she enjoys gardening and walking in the woods, and has a mild addiction to the game of platform tennis.